D0358987

Charlie Johnson
in the Flames

By the same author

Fiction

Asya

Scar Tissue

Non Fiction

A Just Measure of Pain: The Penitentiary in the
Industrial Revolution, 1750–80

Wealth and Virtue: The Shaping of Classical Political
Economy in the Scottish Enlightenment

The Needs of Strangers

The Russian Album

Blood and Belonging: Journeys into the
New Nationalism

Isaiah Berlin: A Life

The Warrior's Honour: Ethnic War and
the Modern Conscience

Virtual War: Kosovo and Beyond

The Rights Revolution

Human Rights as Politics and Idolatry

Empire Lite: Nation-building in Bosnia,
Kosovo and Afghanistan

Charlie Johnson in the Flames

Michael Ignatieff

Chatto & Windus
LONDON

Published by Chatto & Windus 2003

2 4 6 8 10 9 7 5 3 1

First published in Great Britain in 2003 by
Chatto & Windus
Random House, 20 Vauxhall Bridge Road,
London SW1V 2SA

Random House Australia (Pty) Limited
20 Alfred Street, Milsons Point, Sydney,
New South Wales 2061, Australia

Random House New Zealand Limited
18 Poland Road, Glenfield,
Auckland 10, New Zealand

Random House (Pty) Limited
Endulini, 5A Jubilee Road, Parktown 2193, South Africa

The Random House Group Limited Reg. No. 954009
www.randomhouse.co.uk

A CIP catalogue record for this book
is available from the British Library

ISBN 0 7011 7607 5

Typeset by SX Composing DTP, Rayleigh, Essex
Printed and bound in Great Britain by
Mackays of Chatham Plc, Chatham, Kent

For Suzanna Zsohar
who believed in him until I did

ONE

When Charlie saw the helicopter, he was sure everything was going to be all right. It settled down in the stubble-bare, garbage-strewn field by the edge of the refugee tents, and it came down so close he had to shield her face with his hands from the cloud of dust and refuse thrown up by the blades. It made Charlie feel young again, like Danang in '71, to see the pair of medics in the open door unsnap their belts, sling out the stretcher and break into a low crouching run beneath the rotors. They had their helmets on, two young American faces behind flip-down glasses, and the 6th Navy flashes on their shoulders. It was ridiculous, Charlie knew, but there he was, tears in his eyes, at the thought that they were safe in the arms of the empire.

They knelt beside her and one checked the drip that Jacek had been holding above her, giving him the thumbs-up for his work, while the other assessed her vital signs, fingers on the vein in the throat, eyes on the watch, followed by a quick glance, unreadable behind the shades, to his buddy. Then he pulled back the dressing across the top of her back and gave the wound a look of expressionless assessment. They didn't bother with Charlie's hands, bandaged up so that he felt like a kid in mittens four sizes too big. It was great how fast they were, how they concentrated on the essentials, how they lifted her on to the stretcher with that practised combination of moves, one two three, which turned care into procedure. Then they were running low for the chopper, with Charlie flapping behind, his hands held out in front of him and Jacek half holding Charlie so he wouldn't lose his balance.

They fixed a radio helmet on Charlie's head because he couldn't do it himself, and they strapped him in, next to the stretcher, and the medic made a 'No' sign to Jacek who looked desolate but stood back, crouched low and turned away. As they lifted off, the stretcher locked in place by the door and Charlie in the jump-seat beside it, all he could do was wave his panda hands at Jacek below, diminishing and turning, as the helicopter gained height, his lanky blond hair flying about in the rotor chop, alone in the field.

All through the long night, she had moaned and moved her head from side to side, but now she was silent and her eyes were shut. He supposed that she was no longer in pain, that her capacity for pain had been seared away. One medic had pulled back the singed cotton material of her dress from an undamaged section of her left arm and was giving her an injection. Another pulled out Jacek's drip and fitted a new one. The clear fluid rose, delivering salts and glucose into her veins.

Out on the field he hadn't noticed, but inside the helicopter it became apparent that she didn't smell good. It was a complex aroma of womanhood, sweat, urine and the sweetness of singed meat. They couldn't clean her up *en route*, and there was nothing to say that they weren't already saying on the radio back to base.

Over the headphones he could hear the chatter and drew comfort from their military voices: female, twenty to twenty-five, civilian, third degree on twenty-five per cent, no further estimate of injury until examination, then the vital signs, a bunch of numbers for pulse rate and blood pressure that didn't mean anything to Charlie, and some more traffic about preparations for her arrival. It all felt good: they were waiting for her, Navy trauma specialists in a gleaming white theatre.

Charlie wanted to tell her all this, but they shared no language and the chopper noise made communication impossible. They were scudding and shuddering in and out of the cloud banks, and when her eyes opened again they were shiny glimmers in the changing light. She gazed up at the grey-green insulation jacket covering the inside of the chopper, took in the flexes of the radio lines that went into their helmets and jounced as the machine buffeted its way northwards. Then she looked at him and held his gaze, expressionless. He hoped she knew her salvation was now only minutes away. He reached down to her uncharred hand and held it again between his bandaged hands.

All they had in common was the knowledge of what they had been through. But that was enough. Even if they could have spoken, they didn't need to. Now at the end of her ordeal, with deliverance finally at hand, the shock was causing her gaze to blur. Her eyes closed and Charlie removed his hand to edge away, because the smell was beginning to make him gag. He took gulps of air through his mouth and turned his face to the window.

They – or rather Jacek – had done what they could: the IV drip, the bandages from the first aid kit, tied on to her back with strips torn from Jacek's T-shirt. They called in the helicopter with the satellite phone and then they sat by the Jeep all night and waited. In the stupor of pain, Charlie held her hand because he didn't know what else to do. There was an agonising wait for the daylight to come and the weather to clear. We're air-ready, flight control kept saying over the sat phone, but we don't have the ceiling. Fuck air-ready. Fuck ceiling. Get it here! he shouted and slammed the sat phone down. Charlie's penchant for righteous rage normally left him feeling exalted, like George C. Scott playing Patton, but this time whacking down the receiver hurt his hands so much that he had cried out. After that, Jacek took the phone away and whether it was Jacek's Polish patience or his prayers, they got lift-off clearance pretty soon. Deliverance was only an hour away, and it was the real deal, top of the line American trauma medicine, all in tents at the airfield. Charlie knew the place: a month before he'd interviewed some Jordanian peacekeepers who'd walked into a minefield and were being stitched back together there. The ones who could talk, the ones who were more than bandaged stumps of meat held in this life by a breathing pump and a heart machine, had all told him that the doctors were the best. So she would have the best too.

When they got to safety, and she was better, he would tell her how fine she had been, burned and tattered as she was, clambering and stumbling up the track in the dark from the valley where her house had been, to the woods on the other side of the border, at the edge of the refugee camp. She gave out only once, just slipped back without a sound and fell down on the path like a dropped shawl. Charlie couldn't do anything because of his hands but Jacek and Benny linked wrists and carried her, chair-lift, for more than a mile till they got to the level. Jacek had been beyond compare, wordless, teeth clenched, bearing her weight. As for Benny, well Benny could carry a body uphill in the dark for all eternity. When they put her down, she stayed standing, and she just kept on walking straight ahead, along the path, as if she knew safety lay in only one direction.

She would have known the track well. It started right across the road from her house, in the woods at the end of her village. Before the war, there wouldn't have been dogs, snipers and patrols. This was just a trail, one of the dozens that the herders used. When the war came, she would have heard the fighters – her fighters – taking the path at night, down from the plateau on the other side of the border filing past her house to take on the blue half-track and the militia squads in the valley. So now, in her extremity, she must have thought: my knowledge will save me. I will lead these foreigners and keep them to the path and, at the top, someone will stop this pain. So, after Jacek and Benny had put her down she walked ahead of them all, a woman in tatters leading them to safety in the dark.

She had been too shocked, too possessed by pain to look back. Her house was burning to the ground, her village was in flames. Charlie knew what it was that she should be spared, what she should never have to see: the way the hands would clutch the face, and the body would cower and tuck its legs in upon itself in vain search for protection from the flames. If she had seen him like this, her own father, she might have lain down and given up. Instead she kept walking upwards with the foreigners. They kept giving her water and she just kept walking. They hadn't thought she could make it, but she had.

She had run from the house towards the woods where Charlie, Jacek and Benny were hiding, running with her arms outstretched, with the fire on her back flaring like a cloak. Hair on fire, back on fire, dress on fire, flames clinging to her while she ran. He jumped into the road to stop her because he knew – with lunatic clarity – that running was a mistake. Running fans the flames. You never run when you're on fire, every book tells you that, you flatten out, roll in the dust. So he stepped into her path to stop her and she ran right into him, so that they rolled together in the red dirt of the road until they were one crumpled roll of melded flesh, Charlie beating on her back with his hands to douse the flames. As if he, Charlie Johnson, had been chosen by her embrace and anointed like her with the flames. He knew he was crying out, and when he next opened his eyes, she was lying on top of him, stinking of gasoline and burned skin. She was shaking, and he was too, and they kept still, knowing that the squad might still be at the end of the road. He thought that if they did not move someone might take them for dead. He was aware enough to feel that their bodies were transmitting identical intimations of fear. He could hear the flames from the burning roofs and shouts and the pop-pop of small arms. They were so tightly entwined that he could not see her face, but he could hear her moaning next to his ear.

And then Jacek crossed his line of sight, running low with the camera skimming the ground. He flung himself down ten feet away and began to turn over: the house burning, the blue half-track reversing and disappearing out of sight around the bend, all filmed through the wobbly alembic of fear. When Jacek had the shot, he pulled the cassette, jammed it into his pocket and ran over to get them to their feet and into the woods before the patrol returned. Only the patrol didn't return. Darkness swung the advantage their way. The squad would not risk an ambush. Charlie knew they could now move out and take the woman with them, back the way they came. Only later, when they were on the plateau waiting for the helicopter, Charlie realised that Jacek had done something he had never done in their many years of working together: he'd left a camera behind.

All the way up the track, Charlie had thought that she might die. But now it seemed just as obvious that she would survive. People did. There was no reason this had to spin out of control. Looking down, he could see the lights of the airfield and he could feel the chopper coming down fast.

Soon there would be clear water and clean sheets. Surgical scissors would cut the singed garments off her body. Nurses would apply salves and ointments, ice packs to bring down the temperature of the skin. Fluids and plasma would perfuse her veins and she would sleep. She would awake and he would be there to make sure that she was all right. She would get grafts and have months of treatment, courtesy of the US Navy. She couldn't go back, because her village had been torched and her father was gone. But she would be alive, and she was young, and that was something.

As for Charlie, he knew he was finished. For thirty years he had been fucked around by rogues and chancers and drugged-up hoods at checkpoints from Kabul to Kigali, but none of them had ever laid a glove on him, not really. He had heard the bullets whine over his head but in all that time he had never believed any of them were meant for him. He had seen the flames and always believed they would not touch him. Until that afternoon. When he pulled his hands away to see that they were covered with the carbonised remnants of her flesh and his own. Afterwards, waiting for the helicopter, he had sat in the dark, shaking from head to foot, so fully given over to fear that there seemed nothing left of him but terror. Yes, he was finished.

He had left Jacek behind and he was too tired to care. You weren't ever supposed to leave crew behind, and the bureau wouldn't let him forget that, even if it hadn't been his fault. He had not been a hero, and the thought did not bother him in the slightest. If you didn't know what fear was, you were in no position to say a thing.

The patrol of blue half-tracks had come in the quiet, with such stealth that Charlie didn't realise they were there until the roof-tops at the far end of the village began to smoulder and burn. It was unbelievable to watch from the safety of the trees while the squad went from house to house, pulling people out, half-dressed, and leading the men away. He had no idea, and probably she wouldn't know how to explain it either, why she had been the one of all the village women who resisted, rushing up to the squad leader, pleading on behalf of her house, her possessions, her father still inside. She had been so vehement she did not even see the green jerry-can arcing behind her until the gasoline slopped over her back.

Charlie saw it all from his hiding place at the clearing's edge. The others in the squad had their balaclavas on, but not the commander. He had taken the cowl off, as if to say: I am the one who makes the fire come. I am the one you will fear. The lighter flicked open in his hand and he touched her back.

He watched her run, even stayed the hand of one of

his men who drew a bead to fire at the back of her head. He let her run. He had all the time in the world. He watched her dance and tear at herself, until he lost sight of her round the bend of the road. Then he got into the half-track and reversed out of the village.

Her hand was limp as he held it and he wondered whether they would ever be so intimate again. It was clear that the scene they had lived through would remain unmastered as long as he lived and that this race to save her would never undo the fact that he had watched it happen and had been unable to stop it.

The helicopter felt for the pad and settled down. The doors were pulled open and they had a gurney right up under the rotors. They lifted her on and a team raced her away along the tarmac, and two medics were holding him by the elbows, until he shook them away. Everyone left him alone after that. He said he would walk, and they left him to follow the team that was running the gurney into emergency. He could see the low caterpillar shape of the mobile naval hospital, the brown network of tents where they worked on mine victims and emergency medical evacuations from the zone. The air was cold and scented with jet fuel. The interdiction flights were running twenty-four hours a day. In the distance, at the far end of the runway, the Nighthawks were poised for take-off, their fantails glowing crimson. He felt the fear ebbing from him with every step he took. He could see the nurses just ahead, in the light of the halogen arcs at the admission bay of the hospital, taking her inside.

He followed her down the low corridors, lit by sloping arches of 40-watt bulbs, conscious now, as he passed the young surgeons in their theatre scrubs and the naval orderlies in their browns, that he was dirty and blood-soaked and unwell. But they stopped him when the gurney was wheeled into the surgery bay, behind two plastic flanges that closed against him. Two medics sat him down, and a nurse poured sweet milky coffee down his throat, which stopped him shaking, and they attended to his hands. They laid him down on a bed and they put him on a drip, and a blonde nurse, with her mouth covered in hospital green, had his hands on her lap, cleaning them with swabs. Everything hurt, and he said so, and she gave him an injection and he felt nothing at all and lay on his back watching night moths slam their heads into the rows of naked bulbs that snaked down the apex of the tent. The heat ventilators were roaring and the tent flaps were billowing, and dust from the moths' damaged wings filtered through the light and Charlie felt he had made it home and dry. He was lying back with his eyes open, when a young surgeon in scrubs came in. He wanted to know whether he knew her, and Charlie asked, 'What do you mean?' and he said that the female civilian was DOA – or shortly thereafter, he corrected himself – and that since he was going to have to process her, he had to know her name.

'She didn't have one,' Charlie said. For the rest of his life he was to wonder why he had ever allowed himself to believe it would end in any other way.

Two

Charlie was on the bed in the Esplanade, propped up on the pillows, wrapped in a towel. Etta was beside him. Her skin was damp from the shower and smelt of a face cream he didn't recognise. 'What is this stuff?' he said, reaching up with his bandaged hand to touch her cheek. 'Can't remember,' she said. She was in a hotel dressing gown and she had pulled up the pillows behind her. It was well after midnight. He had been talking from almost the moment she arrived. She said, 'Go on.'

Benny had driven the Jeep to the edge of the plateau where the long ravine down into the valley began. It was two in the morning, they had given the competition the slip, and if they did this right, they would be back in the bar for breakfast, with the other crews none the wiser. They left everything they could – lights, batteries, extra tape and medical kit – in the Jeep. The path, about fifty yards from where they parked, dropped steeply and they went down single file, listening to each other's breathing and the sound of their boots on the stones. They couldn't use any light, so they stumbled and grabbed for the low branches and swore. Yes, he had been scared and depressed as well.

'Why depressed?' she asked, reaching over to the cigarette pack on the night table. She didn't smoke, but he did when he felt like this, and she lit it for him and put it between his lips and then took it away.

Before the war began, when the border was patrolled by the international monitors, he told her, Charlie had seen pictures of one of the rebel incursion units that had walked into trouble, when they were infiltrating down into the valley. Some cold-eyed guy from the internationals' forensic unit had taken Polaroid after Polaroid up close. Charlie had run through twenty-eight of the pictures, including one of a woman, good-looking in her camouflage, with brown hair and a shocked expression, as well she might have, since she had walked right into the ambush and would not have seen anything except some muzzle flash in pitch blackness before she felt her life fly out of her chest like a bird.

So yes he was scared, and when he got scared, he got depressed. It was adolescent to court danger at his age. Danger had to have some necessity to it and there was no real necessity here. They were crossing the border, in the middle of a war, going down into the valley, just to file some tape showing that the border villages weren't held by the other side, as they claimed, but by Benny's people. It was a 'good story'.

'Good stories pay for my house,' was Jacek's line. The prince of cameramen, melancholy, withdrawn, with the loping gait of a hunter, and stringy blond hair like a dog's ears that came down to meet the collar of that battered brown leather jacket. Charlie blinked: he knew he was not functioning properly if the thought of Jacek tore him up.

So they were going down the ravine in the dark, on the wrong side of the border, because it was a good story, because all the crews at the refugee camp had been looking for a way to do it and no one finally had the balls to go for it except them. And yes, precisely because they were the oldest crew in the bar, the one with the most miles on the clock, balls had been allowed to decide the question. That was what he was trying to explain to her: from the night in the bar when he and Jacek had drunk too much and Benny had said, 'You don't believe me, I'll take you,' well you had to go.

'Why?' she said.

'Santini was in the bar too.'

'So?'

Her scepticism was unanswerable. Santini's presence should not have made a difference. But it had. It was a case of animal dislike – of Santini's custom-tailored safari jacket, his enraging neatness, and yes, let's admit it now, his youth – making you do stupid things. Fear of being thought ridiculous was a major reason why men did ridiculous things. Charlie knew this and nonetheless had done something that had been a lot more than ridiculous. 'You figure it out,' he said. She said nothing, which was good, since he wasn't in a mood to be told what a fool he had been.

He put some blame for it on the American Bar. An absurd name for an absurd place. It stood a half-mile from the refugees' tents and the stand-pipes and the women pulling up their trousers after a trip to the slit trench. The bar was down a stinking alley, and it had an improbable garden, someone's idea of an oasis, laid down in crazy-paving, which they kept hosing down, and a little fountain, and heavy pine trees all around it shielding it from the squalor of the town. Strewn around the garden on those white chairs were the same foreign news crews night after night, drinking poison and not even pretending to know what they were waiting for. All the refugee stories, the heart-warming, heart-rending stuff had been done and they couldn't cover the war because the war was all but invisible. You could hear the Nighthawks, and sometimes you could see the detonations and once or twice a week they'd be close enough to shake the ground, but otherwise Charlie thought he might as well be back at the bureau watching it on the monitors.

The guy they called Benny hanged around the bar, fixing for the crews. It wasn't his real name and he thought it was beneath his dignity, but everybody called him that. He had been a waiter in Dortmund and Charlie's first instinct was that he was useless. He was always uncomfortable, boasting, trying to pretend he was a player. Jacek thought that he wasn't useless, just someone who couldn't bear to admit that he would rather be in Dortmund, where nothing happened, than here, where his so-called people were fighting for their so-called freedom. 'He is embarrassed to be afraid' was Jacek's considered opinion and this meant that Benny was to be trusted simply because his failings were visible, 'like the rest of us', Jacek added, letting this Polish Catholic thought trail upwards into the pall of smoke which stayed trapped by the pines around the crazy-paved haven of the American Bar.

Benny had established his credibility with the fighters by smuggling in a couple of Uzis from Germany. He talked about his homeland down in the valley, but really, if he had been honest, home was in Dortmund. His German was perfect, and when he had drunk some, he told them about his German woman and their *Kinder*, the municipal *Schwimmbad* at the end of his street, and the good money he was going to make when he could open a place of his own. Or some such thing. They were drinking after all, and Charlie couldn't remember all the nonsense they said, although now it seemed to matter, since it was in that bar that the decision was taken. After a week of Benny talking and not delivering, he came back one night whispering that the brigade commander had 'authorised' him to lead them down to 'the command post', four miles down the track at the edge of the first village in the valley.

'God almighty,' Charlie said, and Etta took the cigarette from his lips and stubbed it out.

Charlie lay beside her, so close he could hear the intimate sounds her body made, the soft rise and fall of her breath. It was all very comforting and yet unsettling, since Charlie had taken a chance on her and they hadn't ever been like this, and they should have been exploring each other's every pore instead of lying side by side, presuming an intimacy that wasn't there at all.

He'd just phoned her. Like that. It was one more thing he'd done that didn't make sense, but which seemed logical at the time. What made him go through with it was that she didn't sound surprised. She hadn't said Why me? Why there? Are you sure? She'd just said, I heard. Are you all right? And he had said, Why? Do I sound funny? You do, she said and he had admitted that he was not quite right.

She'd flown from London to be there. That was something. He was grateful when she showed up in the lobby. When he said so, she replied, 'I don't like grateful. Makes me feel like Mother Teresa.'

'Is glad better?'

She kissed him in the elevator gently on his lips. It was the first time she had ever kissed him. She didn't say anything about the bandages on his hands.

He had stayed in the hotel about half a dozen times, and after his night in the Navy hospital it was where he wanted to be. It had Third Reich corridors, curving, carpeted, high-ceilinged and dim. There was some story about it being a German HQ during the Second World War. So it had shameful glamour in its past and the staff pretended they remembered him, and that was all Charlie wanted in a hotel.

'What are we doing?' Charlie suddenly asked her.

'We're just talking, Charlie,' she said. Charlie thought that sounded all right. It struck him, while he lay there, that he knew so little about her, except that she was from that border region where Ukraine, Hungary and Slovakia met and where there were, or used to be, Jews and Slovaks and Hungarians and Ukrainians all mixed together. That was what she said, leaving you to figure out which one she was. There was the accent, and the smell of her face cream, and the close-fitting cut of her suits, but nothing about her had ever come sharply into focus until that moment when he had checked himself in and reached for the phone, knowing that she was the one he had to call. She hadn't asked the obvious questions like why he hadn't gone home to Elizabeth. Her willingness to let obvious questions go had been impressive. Frankly, he just hoped that she would keep listening and not care whether this had any future. He didn't want to rejoin his life. He hoped his life would stay on the other side of the rain that kept falling in the hotel courtyard and that it would keep raining, and that they could keep hearing it through the white curtains which rose and fell in the breeze.

'Go on,' she said.

It had taken two hours in the dark to get down to the

bottom of the valley. They broke the cover of the trees, where the path gave out on a dust-covered road that ran through the length of the village. There were maybe fifteen houses, although he couldn't see them all because of the bend in the road. They climbed over some low stone fences and then ducked under a clothes-line. By the wall of the first house they stood stock-still, waiting for the sound of their own footfalls to settle, listening to the animals shifting in the straw behind the wooden staves of a barn. In an upstairs window, there was a flicker of someone moving, as if they had been seen. A quarter-moon scudded in and out behind dirty clouds. They heard the Prowlers and F16s above them and they hoped their thunder covered their sounds. Jacek was loping along, keeping low. They hadn't blackened their faces – it wasn't smart to pretend to be a combatant – so they shone like lanterns whenever the moon came out from behind the clouds.

Benny was lost and was trying to pretend he wasn't; straight down the lane, in plain sight. The rebel command post they were supposed to be heading for was nowhere to be seen and the lane was petering out, and they were losing the time they needed to get back up to the plateau before the first patrols.

At the last house in the village – just before the woods closed in again – Benny stopped and they all stepped into the shadow by the barn wall and he tapped on the door. Unbelievably, he seemed to be asking for directions.

That had been the basic mistake, Charlie thought, to have drawn them in, those two people whose names he never knew, to have drawn them into all the consequences. It need not have happened.

But you didn't have time to think because Benny was

beckoning through the open door and they blundered into the room, heavy figures taking up too much space, making too much noise. There were people there, but you couldn't see them, and then hands – Benny's maybe, maybe somebody else's – were pushing you along a passage and down some stairs. The smell of earth and mould and damp told you it was the cellar. And you stayed there listening to the floorboards creak above your head, and Jacek's laboured breathing and the thump of your blood.

It was a rootcellar, not high enough to stand straight up in, dirt on the floor, and somewhere in the dark, onions. But they did not move, just stayed there, framed in dawn light from the window, listening to the noises overhead.

Then they went still. No patrols till six had been Benny's promise, and there it was in the lane, the blue half-track, at ten to five. You heard it before you saw it: a low engine noise, and then through the cobwebbed window, you could see the studded track of its tyres maybe fifteen feet away. You could hear boots stepping down from the half-track, footfall on gravel. So you stood still breathing in the acrid odour of Benny's sweat in the darkness, watching while Jacek edged his face away from the window light into the shadow, then stood motionless, breathing in and out, praying to the Black Madonna of Czestochowa.

Above you, stillness, not even the sound of weight being shifted from one foot to another. The people upstairs, waiting in the dark.

Incredible mental alertness: you had time to think about whether your footprints were still visible on the dusty track, whether the militia had picked them up. You had time for all the possibilities – Benny has betrayed you, he has not; he will buckle, he will not. All the possibilities run through your mind, except of course what happens.

Charlie got up in his towel, went over to the curtains, pushed them aside and watched the rain for a while. He came back to bed, lay down, leaning against her shoulder. She smiled but he had a bad feeling about it: what was he doing here? Why was he leaning against the shoulder of a woman he didn't really know?

'Go on,' she said and Charlie shook his head.

'It's good to talk. But why exactly? Why is it supposed to make any difference at all?'

'You asked me to come,' she said.

'I don't know why.'

'I know you don't. But it doesn't matter.'

'Why are we doing this?'

'Charlie.' It was the way Jacek used to say it, just to shut him up. It worked this time. Someone had to help him stop these futile gusts of helpless self-recrimination. He came back to himself. He thought: she is all right. Isn't investing too much in being here, isn't holding her breath, doesn't want anything from me.

Would *he* have flown from London to listen to this? Not without something in return. Like sloshing around in the bath together, like spilling the minibar over each other and licking it off. But there hadn't been anything like that. In fact, there had been nothing at all. She took a shower. He took a shower. She re-bandaged his hands with the dressings the Navy had given him. She unpacked a small bag and hung a dress in the closet. She tossed his clothes into a hotel laundry bag, rang for service and told them to dispose of them and to send for new ones, same size, in the city. He watched all this with approval. She took charge. He liked that. The weather lifted inside him and he knew all he had to do was lie there with her and talk it out, talk it through until it was no longer weighing upon his chest.

Etta was what he would have called an office friend, though he didn't know what to call her now. She had been there when he took the job at the bureau, and for a long time he didn't pay her any attention. She didn't go out on the road. She was there when he came back. She was Etta the unit manager, famously efficient, famously unapproachable, famously gone at six sharp every evening. She had outlasted four editors, the smart boys, she called them. Charlie's contempt for management was unruly and professionally suicidal, while hers had a queenly disdain which he came to admire.

He had said to her once that she should be running a small country. She laughed and then said in her dark voice, 'No, Charlie, it is enough to run you.' So she stayed: they all got younger, except Charlie and her. He supposed they were about the same age though with women you could never be sure. She was the subject of much speculation, most of it sexual, because of the perfume and a couple of cream outfits that made even soundmen, the most boring train spotters in their business, sit up and sniff the office air like hungry dogs. But because she was Eastern European, and 'kept to herself' and was older than most of the crews, nobody had tried anything, or come back to tell about it. She knew everything of course because she processed all the expense claims. What male sordidness was there in those piles of chits: trips to brothels, doctor's bills for the clap, hard-core services of every description, which they dropped on her desk, followed by comical, bold-facing lying, about why none of it looked as bad as it seemed.

Charlie had tried it on a few times himself, but she was never fooled. She listened expressionless and then tossed back two of his claims just to let him know that she was not taken in by his low-rent villainies.

They had become friends, but he couldn't remember when. Not at first, but slowly over the years. He would sit on the edge of her desk, pass her a cup of coffee from the machine and that was when he got used to talking to her, got used to her kind of listening, which was intent and detached and seemed to know where he was going before he got there. He would tell her about the assignments, and because she'd done the flights and hotels, hired the fixer, she understood. She knew where you could get a decent camera in Peshawar or Luanda or whatever, and had once hired a plane which extricated him from Kigali when nobody was landing there. Her competence back at the fort came to be something he depended on in the field. You could tell your story quickly and she didn't need a lot of explanation. So a certain complicity had developed. One-sided, he now realised, because he didn't talk about home and she never ventured the slightest hint about her private life. The one time he took a step into that terrain, asking what she was doing that weekend, she replied, looking up over her glasses, 'That is none of your business.' And then she threw him out because she had too much paper, she said. 'Get out, Charlie. Come back some other time. I'm busy now.'

Then there came the day he returned from the funeral in the States. She stopped him in the corridor to say that he didn't look so good, and he walked into her office and slumped in the seat in front of her desk. He told her about his dad, a lieutenant in the Army Corps of Engineers, out of Des Moines, six foot four and a half in his stocking feet, who had liberated the camp, with Mika in it, in Wiesbaden, Germany, in 1945. He had taken Mika back to Dedham, Mass., where he turned her into an American and gave her a sense that the world would always be steady under their feet, until the Sunday morning when Mika found him by the work-bench, every spanner, wrench and screwdriver still in its place on the wall, lying on the garage floor, dead of a heart attack at sixty-three. If Charlie thought about it now, Frank's passing was the beginning of the bad period, for Mika had nestled like a bird in Frank's arms for forty years. When he was no longer there, she soon ceased to be there either, which was why their son, Charles Johnson, who had gone to war like his father and trusted to his strength as much as she had, sat in Etta's office and found himself swallowing his tears.

You could explain their being in the hotel together, he thought, by this history of confession, except that you wouldn't want to exaggerate. Apart from that one time, talking about the death of both of his parents, there hadn't been all that much confessing.

There was a lot she did not know, like, for example, why he had called her, and not his wife, when the Navy hospital had discharged him. He didn't either. So that made two of them. They were there in the hotel, waiting until the reason became obvious to both of them, and he would either return to his life or blow it up.

'You are in the rootcellar, Charlie,' she said.

The squad didn't come through the door, not then anyway. The half-track moved on slowly with its treads making a clinking sound like hot coals slipping down in a grate. Nobody moved, not in the cellar, not in the house above. It was like that for hours. They did nothing but sit there, once moving over to the pile of onions to piss, which left them stuck with the smell of their urine and the onions mixing together in the dirt.

A man could die of restlessness. If you believed you had to take charge of all the waiting – that was the way to get yourself wasted. That day he learned from Jacek how to wait: to go into a special Polish Catholic zone of attentive motionlessness, waiting for the sun to make its transit of the dirty window, watching the blades of grass flame as the sun went through them.

But the people in the house went out. From the cellar window, Charlie couldn't see more than an old man and the woman, who must have been his daughter, working in the vegetable patch. The patrol came by twice. If the old man and the woman were hiding the presence of the strangers in their rootcellar, they were doing a terrific job. If they were about to betray them, they were also doing a terrific job. Charlie had no idea what was going to happen.

The light was fading, and the cover of a possible escape was coming up rapidly when Benny flicked on the radio and whispered his call sign. Jacek leaned his head against the cellar wall and closed his eyes. 'Idiot,' he whispered. Exactly. As if the patrols weren't monitoring every band. Then there was a scratchy reply, low but distinct. So now they had to move, because the patrols would be back, zeroing in on where Benny's signal came from.

Benny went first, beckoning them up from the cellar and giving them the run sign, and they hurtled down the short passage to the light, clearing the village track and blundering into the trees the other side. When they reached the woods, Charlie turned and looked back:

there were eyes watching him from the window of the house.

'We shouldn't have left them.'

'It happened too fast,' she said.

She was not there to pronounce absolution. But then it occurred to him it wasn't she who was interested in absolution. It was him.

Benny hadn't been *that* wrong, just five hundred yards wrong, and they found the rebel command post on the first ridge among the pines, within sight of the house. Except that 'command post' was ridiculous for just a dug-out so well hidden that it might have been a trap for animals. There were three of them, village boys, absurdly young and not exactly inspiring confidence, but they had face camouflage which made them look like semi-serious killers and in the forest gloom Charlie could see RPGs, Zastavas and some armour-piercing shells on a clip. Jacek was happy because he could turn over and Charlie did a breathless stand-up, in the dug-out, trying to project enough sound volume to get picked up on the camera mike, but not enough to get them caught, with the red-rimmed eyes of the fighters just visible at the rear of the shot. Looks real, Jacek said, after he had checked the gate, except that Charlie knew it wasn't especially real. The camera always had a way of flattening things out, leaching the danger out of any moment. Danger or not, it was a good career move. Charlie had a report proving that the guerrillas were still active in villages within four miles of the border. And the twenty-somethings were still dozing in the American Bar. Now all they had to do was get it up the hillside when the darkness came, reach the sat phone in the Jeep and beam it back.

'So Shandler could pass you in the hall and give you his significant nod,' Etta said.

24

'Fuck Shandler. And his significant nod,' Charlie said.

He slowly slipped down so that he was lying with his head in her lap. She did not play with his hair; she did not stroke his chin or rub her hand along his eyebrows. She let him use her lap: that was all. And she would stick a cigarette between his lips from time to time. His palms hurt and when he went to scratch them against each other, she stopped him. 'You were lucky,' the surgeon said. 'All you needed to lose was another fraction of an inch, and you'd have been in trouble.' A half-second more. The terrifying unworthiness of good luck.

Etta asked if he had seen Jacek's footage, but he shook his head. There was a television in the room, but he didn't even want to watch the competition. Santini was probably down there right now. The blood would draw the flies.

They thought it was going to be all right, the three of them sitting there in the dug-out with the village boys, waiting for another half-hour more of darkness to cover their escape back up the track to safety. It was amazing to him now, this foolish hopefulness. After almost thirty years in the business, how many times had he been shot at? How many times had he and Jacek put their noses above some wall and made a calculation: Do we run? Do we stay? Which way is the story moving? How far to that wall over there? Everything turned on decisions like that. It was not addictive. That was what people said, who didn't know anything about it. Addiction was not what it felt like, because it didn't feel crazy or out of control. It was about the conviction that a certain kind of experience gave you, or at least what he felt when he and Jacek were assessing the same risk. They just knew. If there was any intoxication in what they did, it was this knowledge, the accumulated experience of two old dogs who had done all their hunting together. Jacek looked the part: the gait, the long nose, the watchfulness, the way he cocked his head when he listened. But all this self-confident knowledge had just evaporated. From now on Charlie wasn't sure of anything. His hands weren't shaking. But they would. He had picked up a tremor, he was sure of it. All the old bastards got it sooner or later. Now it was his turn.

They started out from the dug-out just as the sun set. It was two hours back to the top, more or less, but they only went a hundred yards before they had to take cover. The firing started and they thought it was aimed at them. You always do. But it wasn't. Nothing was coming through the trees. They were perfectly safe. It was down in the village.

The half-tracks, four of them, had returned and the squads were smashing down the doors, pulling the men out into the road, while others were tossing lighted brands inside. Jacek and Charlie watched from the trees while the lead half-track clanked to a stop in front of the house where they had been hidden. The turret swivelled, the gun moving back and forward across the whitewashed stones, the red tiled roof, the garden on the side where the woman and her father had been putting in a spring planting, even tying up an aluminum pie tin on a pole to scare away the birds.

The three of them, in blue-black body armour, went through the front door, and five hundred yards away in the cover of the pines, you could hear the sound of wood being smashed, glass splintering and a scream, muffled through the walls, but so distinct, so piercing, so lonely. You had your face in the dirt and your hands over your ears.

When Charlie looked up, a fourth one in body armour was out of the half-track carrying the jerry-can to the door.

The village boys in the dug-out could have started shooting, but it would have drawn fire, and they were no match for the half-tracks. So they just sat there, as stunned as Charlie and Jacek. She was out in the road by then, running towards the commander, shouting.

Charlie was pacing the hotel room now, and the towel had slipped off his waist. He was naked but for the bandages on his hand, not caring about being ridiculous, he was back there, really back there, with the story inside him needing to be pulled out, like some infected splinter. She watched from the bed.

One member of the squad with a jerry-can was sloshing down the door-frames and windows, the garden fence, the plants, the grassy path to the door. She was screaming at the commander, fists raised, when the gasoline arced over her and the lighter touched her hem. She went up with her house, an orange-black spinnaker of flame catching the wind. Jacek began to turn over, whispering as he stared down the viewfinder, mouthing Polish prayers.

She was running along the road towards them, while the commander watched her go, and stayed the mercy of an executioner's bullet. Then he climbed into the half-track, reversing hard and turning around to finish the operation.

That was when the torpor of fear ended and you broke cover and stepped into the road. As she ran, her arms were like wings of flame, and she blundered into you in an embrace of fire – and you were both down, in the dusty road, rolling over and over.

They had ten minutes maybe, before the patrol came

back. The village boys might cover them, might not. You remembered pulling her off and sitting up, looking at your hands and then at her, legs and lower body intact, but shoulders and upper arms charred and that terrible place across the top of her back. Jacek had his water bottle out and poured it across her shoulders and she cried out.

Only Jacek had instincts you could trust. Benny was shaking, and talking to himself, and Jacek told him to get her up if she could walk, which she could, and get her into the trees. She did not look back at the burning house. Her father was in there, but it was too late.

He remembered Jacek taking Benny by the shoulders and shaking him and saying: we are taking her. When Benny said they couldn't, Jacek told him to shut up. And then they poured water down her throat and down her back, and she said nothing, and seemed to feel nothing, and fell, and Benny and Jacek picked her up and carried her most of the way, and she astonished them by walking ahead of them, like a possessed spirit, the final mile to the edge of the plateau where, reaching safety, she buckled again. Behind came Charlie stumbling and falling, reaching out to the trees and crying out when his singed hands rasped against the bark. And all along the road, they had one thought: it will be all right if we can get her to the other side. And then it was: it will be all right if we can get her into the chopper. And then it was: it will be all right if we . . .

He was now standing in the middle of the hotel room, looking at his hands. Weak light came through the windows and the sound of rain.

'What am I doing here?'

He was crying, ignominious and naked, waving his

useless hands to and fro, as if he thought this would take the burning away.

'What am I doing?'

Etta came to him and stood there in front of him. Then she undid her robe and he stepped closer and she folded him in. She said nothing, just held him and he held her with the weight of his wrists against her shoulders and his bandaged palms out a fraction from her body. They stood like that for a long time.

THREE

He began to shiver so she put him into bed and covered him up, his bandaged hands out flat on his chest. She went to the bathroom and when she came back some minutes later he was asleep, mouth open, looking old and vulnerable. She lay down beside him and watched him sleep, then slept herself, then woke and in the warmth of the bed and his body next to hers, she kissed him. The bedside light was still on, and she saw his eyes open as her lips came down on his. He reached for her, but she laughed softly and pushed his hand away and said, 'Let me.'

She came down astride him and held his hands back against the pillows so he would not be tempted to help. As she made love to him, there was guileless candour in his eyes. It astonished them both that this was possible, after what had happened to him, and as the known yet unquenchable pleasure rose within her, Etta felt that the rain-bounded night was lifting and that the room's confines had suddenly opened out on to a future together. She knew a lot about hope, and she knew how to keep it under control, but just then it was seductive.

When Charlie woke a few hours later she was sitting

in the chair on the other side of the room, holding a cup of tea and looking out the window. He lay watching her. The scent of her body was on his skin and in the sheets. With men, like with Jacek, you could tell what they were thinking. But with women, you never knew. He was thinking – where the hell do we go from here? – but right away, he knew that she was not. She came over, sat on the edge of the bed, gave him some of her tea and when he seemed fully awake, Etta said, 'How did you leave her?'

On a slab in the surgical tent, exposed, alone, denuded. Then rolled off the slab into a body bag and then . . . Jesus. He reached for the phone but she got there first and dialled the hospital and held the phone to his ear while he sat up in bed.

The male duty nurse on the 6th Navy hospital switchboard told Charlie that the female civilian, not having any next of kin, had been incinerated. He corrected himself, had been cremated. And the ashes? Charlie wanted to know. These were operational details. Charlie replied that they weren't goddamned operational details. The woman was . . . and here he faltered, choosing between alternatives, none of which were satisfactory – she is my kin, she is my friend and so on –, settling on 'I was with her when she died', which hadn't been true either. The duty nurse said he understood, sir, and he was sorry, but there was nothing he could do about it, because the ashes had already been disposed of. Charlie began shouting that this wasn't the fucking point, the fucking point was – at which Etta put the phone down.

Charlie was striding around the hotel room, shouting that they hadn't even kept her ashes or effects, such as they were: a carbonised dress, one shoe, possibly an earring or a ring, though he couldn't remember whether she had been wearing any jewellery. Etta said she doubted there would have been any, but Charlie didn't seem to be listening. Whatever there had once been, it was all disposed of. He was working himself up into a tirade, and she knew what these were like. When Shandler had told him the assignment to Kabul was going to someone else, he had stormed back to his office, picked up a full glass bottle of Perrier and hurled it at the dartboard hanging on the back of his office door. She came and stood in the doorway and told him to stop being a child and he had laughed and kicked the glass at his feet back in her direction. Now he was striding around the room, declaiming at the thoughtless horror of modern life – those black plastic body bags, the industrial incinerators for human beings, the stainless steel sluice bays, the rubber gloves, the whole infernal machinery in which a human being was reduced to nothingness – when she said that he should get dressed and stop talking.

He did so silently, feeling as if he had just been slapped. She put a shirt over his shoulders, pulled his hands through the sleeves, fastened the buttons. As she handed him his underpants and trousers, and steadied him as he put them on, she smiled at him to lighten him up, trying to get him to remember that there had been happiness just the other side of sleep, and that they must not lose it. But from his hooded, dogged look she knew that he was somewhere else. He was watching the woman go through those twin plastic flanges at the end of the tented corridor where the surgeons worked and she had never come out again, and here he was realising – he now said with absurd vehemence – that he hadn't given her a proper Christian burial. Except, Etta added quietly, that she wasn't Christian and they didn't even know her name.

From the way Etta fitted the coat on his back and took him outside into the rain-washed April air, it was clear that she was treating him like a convalescent lunatic. He submitted with dull ill grace, following her to a lugubrious café where they both had a coffee. He sat in a corner booth staring out through the smeared window at the people in the street. She had the antibiotics and the painkillers the Navy had given him in her purse, and she counted one of each out into her hand and made him swallow them with his coffee.

He found himself wondering what Annie was doing at this hour. With the time difference, she would be in assembly, though since he had never been there, not being one of those *perfect* fathers, he didn't know what the assembly hall would be like. He seemed to remember her saying that they had prayers. What prayers? he had asked her, and Annie, using the voice she reserved for her father's dumber questions, had said they were about God and loving people and so on. Thinking about Annie filled him with a sense of weightlessness, as if he was coming untethered. He wanted to talk to Etta about this. Wasn't the feeling of fatherhood supposed to tie you down in this world, give you a sense of belonging to someone? He asked her whether she had ever had any children and she said she hadn't. Why not? Charlie asked, and she said it had just never happened, not wanting to go into the marriage to the German businessman that had got her safely out of her small town at nineteen or the later relationship that brought her to London and eventually to Charlie's office, by this time on her own. Do you miss it? Charlie asked, and she said, Miss what? Having children wasn't essential, it wasn't an answer for anything, still less a way to belong to the world and be at home there. She didn't say all of this, but enough so that Charlie said that he was going to resent all of her wisdom pretty soon.

'God,' she said, 'you have a gift for misery,' suddenly angry that he should be squandering simple happiness. But he looked so depressed when she had said it that she touched the top of his hands and held the pressure there, as if to keep him from sinking any lower. She pulled him up by his elbows and walked him out to the street. She stuck her arm in his and swung her other one free and tried to get him to shed his mood.

'Where are you taking me?' he wanted to know. 'Ever been here before?'

She hadn't but she knew what she was looking for. She led the way with a certainty of purpose which belied the fact that she was actually lost. 'Where are you taking me?' he asked again, irritably.

'We must do something for her,' she said.

The church she found was a dark, peeling, neglected place apparently inhabited only by mice, bats, and old women moving between the candle-stands in front of the saints' pictures, snuffing out dying flames between their fingers. 'Are you religious?' he asked her but she ignored him.

Saint Agnes, Saint Cecile and Saint Catherine stared down at Charlie from the damp walls, oily and lachrymose renderings in smoke-dulled colours, and he felt a keen urge to leave in search of a bar, but she had him firmly by the arm, and they went to a crone dozing by the candle-stands and bought two candles, and she took him into one of the alcoves, heavy with the odour of candle-wax and soot and damp. She lit the candles and then she sat down on a rickety chair and he did too and they watched the two candles, taller than the rest, flicker and burn. All of this – even if renounced – remained in her past somewhere, and it seemed good to him that her instincts would lead her back here. He knew it was sentimental to feel comforted by consolations in which he did not believe, and he did not feel comforted exactly, rather informed, one more layer at a time, about who she was. The agitation in him was stilled, unexpectedly, and he sat beside her and then felt dumb sadness steal over him like the damp.

One candle was for her, the woman he tried to save but couldn't, the woman who never should have died, but did. Who was the other candle for? A blues stole into his head, the one about the two lights on the last car of a receding freight train down a long line of track:

> The blue light was my baby
> And the red light was my mind

In the street outside the church, she said she would take him back to London.

'So I need taking?'

'Look at yourself,' she said.

'How?' he said with a hard smile, turning in the street, his hands outstretched, while shoppers eddied around him, eyeing him with indifferent curiosity.

'I'll tell you then,' she said. 'You look half dead and need a week at home in bed.'

'I don't want to know. How about a drink?' Charlie was looking around for a bar, with an empty, restless look in his eyes.

'I'm on the flight today and so are you,' she said.

'Go without me,' he replied, looking at her straight.

She had come to take him home. He was in no state to be wandering, and she was not here for an adventure.

She didn't care about his wife and child; it was just that she didn't want to collude in folly and end up making him worse than he was. That was when – looking at him in the street, unkempt and surly – she felt she had had enough. When he was like this, with the hard look in his eye, she knew she was powerless to stop him sweeping everything away, all the strands they had weaved together between them in the night, like a man pushing a cobweb off his face.

'I can't stand you like this,' she said.

'Like what?'

'Just looking for a way to do yourself more harm.'

'Etta.' He tried to take her hands, but she wouldn't let him.

He tried again. 'Stay.'

'Charlie, go home. See your child. See your wife. Sort yourself out. Then we'll see. You need to be in bed, and I don't want to play nurse.'

'I don't want a nurse.'

'You did, and now you don't know what you want so I can't help you any more.' She opened her purse, took out his pills and stuffed them into the pocket of his coat.

'Come on, baby.'

She shook her head and turned quickly before he could pull her back. He watched her until she had disappeared round a corner.

That was quick, he thought. She was nothing if not efficient and she was definitely not his baby.

He drank some of the local plum brandy in the nearest bar and when he returned to the hotel, she had checked out. He sat on the unmade bed, feeling pathetic and disliking himself for it. There ought to have been a note, he thought sourly. That's how these things should be done. So he turned over the pillows and then opened the drawers of the bedside table. His hands hurt but he even shook the Gideon Bible. But there was no note. He sat still for a moment, feeling the bad weather inside him, wondering who would change the bandages on his hands.

The phone rang twenty times before Jacek picked it up. 'I was feeding my animals,' he said.

'She didn't make it,' Charlie said.

'I know.'

'What the hell were we thinking?'

'I don't know.'

'How did you get back?'

'We drove.' North up the coast, Charlie knew, where they dropped the Jeep and then a flight home.

'And Benny?'

'Don't talk to me about Benny.'

When Charlie asked whether he could fly out there and stay a few days, Jacek said he had better check with Magda. The phone went down and Charlie sat there listening to the silence in Jacek's world. Then he came back on and said that Magda thought he should go home to Elizabeth first.

Elizabeth. The mention of her name was cold and clarifying. In his mind's eye, he saw her make that familiar gesture of tossing her hair to get it clear when she picked up her flute, turned her eye to the music and began to play. He had seen her do it all their life together, and now for the first time, he realised that she was looking at the music, not at him, never at him. He knew this was a dreary and self-pitying thought – that she had eyes for the music, not for him – but there it was.

How could he explain to Elizabeth what had happened? How could she possibly understand? She was a good woman, and she had been a tender one, so he couldn't walk around pretending he was misunderstood or neglected or whatever it was that other whining hacks liked to say. He had no complaints. It was just that he needed asylum, and the peculiar feature of his home was that it had never offered asylum. Charlie felt impressed, as if a nagging puzzle in a former life had become clear.

'Come on, Jacek, let me come and feed the pigs,' he said. 'Then I'll go home. I promise.'

'Go home first, Charlie. Magda is right.'

'Everybody says I should go home. Why is that?' Charlie asked.

Jacek let that pass. He never bothered replying to Charlie's rhetorical questions. It was one of the best things of their friendship. Another good thing was that when Charlie wanted something bad enough, Jacek knew it was a waste of time to persuade him otherwise. So he said they could feed the pigs together.

At the airport, everyone treated him well. It was because his hands were bandaged. People held doors open for him. They carried his shoulder bag. He should do this more often, he thought, except that his palms had started to hurt and he wanted to tear off the bandages and scratch. There were only two foreign gates in the airport and the London flight was still boarding, and he suddenly found himself hurrying in the direction of that one, but Etta wasn't in the line of those waiting to board, she must already be in her seat. He couldn't call her back, and anyway he didn't know what to say, so he stood by the glass and watched the plane pull back from the stand. Waving would have been stupid, but that was what he wanted to do.

His flight was full and they had him wedged in the middle seat. There was a girl next to him, with an acrid smell about her, and a dozing old lady in the window seat. The girl poured his vodkas for him, because the three little bottles were too much for his hands, and she smiled at him, but they had no common language and so Charlie only had vodka for company, his elbows pinned to his side, knees bumping the seat in front and the headrest burrowing into his fifth cervical disc. He knew it was the fifth cervical because that was where the surgeon had gone in twenty years before. He had a scar to prove it, indeed the only scar on his body. In a morgue it would be what a cop would call a visible distinguishing mark, the way he might still be identified if the rest of him was unrecognisable. Charlie knew that this was a bad train of thought, but short of more vodka, he was stuck with it.

He must have dozed off because when he awoke there was food on the passengers' tray tables on either side of him and the stewardess and the cart were somewhere behind. His vodka bottles were gone too so he sat and felt his hands aching. The girl was eating her way through her salad and then lifted the foil off the hot portion of the meal. It was grilled beef with some kind of a sauce, the meat red, moist and streaked with carbonisation. Charlie shut his eyes, but the smell would not let him go. The plane began bucking and the seat-belt sign came on. The smell of the meat was every-where. He had to get up. Now. Charlie clambered over the girl, grimacing as his hands clutched at the back of her seat, while she let out a cry and grabbed her tray. They were still serving in the aisle, but he pushed by, and though one of the stewardesses tried to stop him, telling him to return to his seat, Charlie got by her and made it safely to the toilet at the back, where he locked himself in and then fell down on his knees. So that was how, in a Polish airliner, with a stewardess banging on the door, and Charlie on his knees, holding the toilet seat with bandaged hands, vomiting into the bowl, he was revisited for the first time, though not for the last, by the sight and smell of the carbonised flesh on the burning woman's back.

FOUR

When he caught sight of Jacek watching him come down the ramp, Charlie knew he must be looking terrible, but since Jacek had often seen Charlie looking terrible, he didn't say anything, just took the bag off his shoulder and led him to the car. Charlie half expected a Saab or something fancy, since he assumed that all those freelance dollars would have made him a Polish millionaire, but it was an old Lada, and it smelt of dog, and Jacek took the windshield wipers out of the glove compartment and fitted them back on and Charlie felt they were back in the 1980s, when he and Jacek had first met.

December 1981 in Warsaw to be exact. General Jaruzelski, the one behind the deadly shades, had declared a state of emergency. Charlie and his crew were there filming as the police turned fire-hoses on the crowd and the water jet caught a woman coming out of a doorway and began spinning her around, drenched and frozen, her handbag ripped out of her hands by the water jet and then falling so that her legs, tights and underwear were visible and the hose man was sweeping her up and down the sidewalk, like a piece of trash being driven down a drain. Fantastic footage is what he thought at the time, the ignoble character of it only striking him later when he watched it back at the bureau. He was debating how much closer his crew should go in, when he caught his first sight of Jacek, a blurred presence at his side, a snapper in a leather jacket photographing the woman skittering about on the pavement, struggling to get up, then being knocked down again, while a sodden crowd watched unable to help her. Jacek edged closer and suddenly he had a garbage can gripped between his hands over his head and was hurling it at the man with the hose, who caught the full force of it and toppled backwards against the water truck. The hose came loose and its brass head began flailing about on the ground. While another cop rushed to turn it off the woman had time to get to her feet and disappear into the crowd, and then the police charged from across the square and they got Jacek and all Charlie could see were their batons coming down in a tight circle around him. When Charlie moved in and began filming the beating, the batons came his way too, and so he ended up in a military hospital, with a cut on his head, explaining himself and waiting to be deported. But not before he had seen Jacek in the same hospital, on a gurney in his sodden jeans and leather jacket, hands on his chest like some medieval tomb sculpture and a serene expression on his face below a large white bloody bandage. He turned to Charlie and gave him a nod of recognition as they took him away.

He did eighteen months for the trick with the garbage can and when Charlie next saw him it was nine years later at a Solidarity meeting in Gdansk shipyard. Jacek was leaning against the back wall of a union hall, ignoring the talk, which never interested him much, and snapping the factory women in smocks who brought the vodka into the meeting without the big guys ever noticing that they were there. He was a good snapper, but it didn't take much for Charlie to persuade him to, as he put it, go into motion pictures. From then on, they were inseparable: Slovenia, summer 1991; Novska and Pakrac, October 1991; Sarajevo, Christmas 1992; Mostar, summer 1993; and on and on: Mogadishu, Luanda and Huambo, Kabul, all the assignments lined up in his mind like so many rows of tape. They were holidays from hell every one of them, and Jacek seemed to survive them by keeping everything contained within the black frame of his viewfinder. It was often all Jacek would say about a bad situation: 'Look,' he would say, having framed up, and then he would gesture at the machine, and Charlie would look through into the digital world and think: Yes, it looks like something when Jacek frames it up. I can deal with this. They'd seen the world together, though they'd seen it too close to know what it really meant. Sometimes they both felt like spectators at a terrible and violent play. Sure, they wanted to go on stage and stop it. But these plays couldn't be stopped.

The worst thing was that their experience got blurred, lost definition, one bad play shading into the next. Everybody said they had interesting lives, which was true, and it seemed pretty stupid to complain, but after a while it just became a series of assignments, a set of stories you told when you got home but which left you with a feeling that their reality had escaped you. 'We suffer from too much experience,' Jacek said once. 'We have more than we know what to do with.' Which was why Jacek began turning down assignments and would disappear to the farm and his pigs, and nobody could reach him. He managed his

43

exposure a lot better than Charlie, and, altogether, he was saner.

Charlie was thinking all this as they hit the four-lane and the windshield wipers came on, and Jacek said nothing and the big German rigs kept passing and slewing rain on to the car with a thump which made the Lada shake. He had no idea where they were going other than it was bound to be the farm but almost anything seemed fine, and Charlie fell asleep in his coat.

It was too dark to see much when they arrived, bucking and weaving along a dirt track, the Lada's headlights playing over the tops of dark wet furrows. It was all new to him, and he realised that never having met Magda before, he had simply presumed that they would both have to take him in. He was asking people to make a lot of allowances, Etta and now these two, and he didn't like what it said about his state of mind, his eerie helplessness. Charlie was going to say all this, but it was too late, for the lights picked out the barn and the white house and now they rolled up to the gravel in front of the door and there in the open doorway, leading back into the kitchen, stood Jacek's wife.

Her hair was up, and she was wearing jeans and what looked like one of Jacek's checked shirts and a pair of white socks on her feet. She had glasses on the end of her nose and she had been cooking. Early forties, he thought. All Jacek ever said about her was that she translated books for a living, ran the farm and was, as he put it once, with fine philosophical precision, 'the principle of my existence'. The minute he saw her Charlie felt bad, for she looked at him with the same appraising look as Etta, only Etta was probably back in London by now and wouldn't want to see him again. Charlie stood there in the kitchen, mute with longing.

44

Magda poured them vodka and they drank by the pots simmering on the stove, under a red light, and Jacek said something to her in Polish. Magda looked at Charlie – gaunt, unshaven, a shirt-tail sticking out, and a stain of vomit on his trouser leg – and said, 'We have a case of post-traumatic stress disorder.' She pronounced the syllables with ironic distinctness, as if to distance herself most of the way, but not entirely, from these American notions. Charlie smiled.

'I don't see it like that,' he said. 'I just didn't want to go home.'

'Why not?' she asked.

'Because I'm not ready,' he replied.

'So we will get you ready,' she said. On that basis, he could see, she could have him here without betraying his wife. Charlie thought he deserved praise for such intuition about the way women's ethical principles worked.

Magda drank her vodka and then disappeared into another room, reappearing with some cotton wool, adhesive and disinfectant. 'For your hands.' He patted his pockets, looking for something, and realised that he had left the Navy pills at the hotel. So here he was, the man he impersonated sometimes but really disliked, the helpless guy. It dawned on him that Etta had been right as usual, he was worse than he thought. But it was too late for Etta now.

FIVE

Magda cut the dressings off his hands and examined the wounds carefully in the light over the kitchen table. The pads of the fingers and the base of both palms were the worst. Charlie looked at the suppurating red zones without interest, but she bent over, sniffed them and made a face. She gripped his hands tightly to hold them still and cleaned each sore with a Q-tip dipped into disinfectant. It hurt and he felt like a kid sitting there across from her watching the intent way she worked. She was a fine-looking woman, Charlie thought, especially the nape of her neck, from the collar of her checked shirt up to the wisps of brown hair that hung down from her hair clip. Charlie wanted to lean forward and kiss her, startle her with the force of his lips against hers. This was not a great idea, with his best and truest friend sitting with a drink in his hands, watching them both from across the room. It was a bad sign to be so susceptible. He was just a bundle of longing, he thought, and it was disreputable to be so. She applied some ointment to the burns and then re-wrapped both hands in bandages. She even took his temperature, and when she took the thermometer away from his lips she said that if he was still like that in the morning she would call the doctor.

Charlie said he needed another vodka, and so they sat around the kitchen table, drinking without a word. The silence was all he needed, Charlie thought, as he listened to the wind at the windows and felt the noble Wyborowa lighting him up inside.

They installed him in the upstairs bed of one of their absent sons, away at college, and Jacek undid Charlie's shirt and helped him pull his trousers off. When Charlie was alone, staring up at low clouds scudding across a skylight above his bed, his hands swollen now and hurting, he thought he might stay here a long time.

When he woke it was mid-afternoon, and there was a carpet of snow on the skylight. Snow in April on the flat Baltic plain was unusual, so he stood at the window and felt lucky. What a great place, he thought. He had trouble pulling on his trousers and his shirt, and his hands were as sore as before, but he didn't think he had a fever.

Downstairs, it was quiet. All the objects seemed to stand separately in their own circle of light: Jacek's Timberland boots, muddy and worn, by the front door, and her slippers next to them; on the table in the kitchen, potatoes in a bowl; in the sink, two dishes which had held soup, in the room where the TV was, a T-shirt, hers, across the couch. Charlie touched it and heard through the half-open door of the room opposite Magda say, 'Charlie?' and caught sight of Jacek's bare foot as it tapped their bedroom door shut.

Charlie went back into the kitchen, got the door of the fridge open with his elbow, and managed to get a pint of milk to his lips. He drank all of it and turned and stood looking out at the snow blanketing the Lada. It was bad to be in the way, Charlie thought, but he didn't know where else to go, so he stood there, leaning against the sink, watching the snow fall.

It was a while before they appeared. Magda was in a blue striped dressing gown, and she smelt good as she brushed by him. She took his hands in hers and turned them palms up, not opening the bandages, just looking at his arms carefully to see if the infection was spreading.

'Were you ever a nurse?' Charlie asked. She shook her head.

'Elizabeth called.'

'That's ingenious of her,' Charlie said, making a face.

'We said you might be here for a few days.'

'Thank you,' Charlie said, wanting to put his head on her shoulder. This whole desire to lay his head anywhere that was soft and female was getting out of control. He smiled and she smiled back.

'The doctor is coming in half an hour. You need antibiotics.'

'I need an alibi.' She moved away and filled the kettle at the sink, looking out at the snow, affectionately, like someone who loved exactly this view and the way the snow had softened and then obliterated the world outside.

Why explain? He didn't want to go home, and since Magda didn't know his wife and his child, she didn't have to know why.

Jacek, also in a dressing gown, padded in, feet bare, sat down at the kitchen table and rubbed his face. When she placed tea in front of him he cupped it with his hands, looking out at the snow. She stood by the window at the kitchen sink and Charlie thought that the way they were together, just then, silently watching the snow fall, looking out at their garden, was the closest approximation of happiness he had seen for a long time. He also thought that it had nothing to do with him, and that he shouldn't be here. They would be happier without him.

Etta had called too. She had been talking to the insurance people, Jacek said, and they weren't happy about it but the camera left behind in the valley would be covered. She'd had to make up some story, but they had bought it. Charlie knew that was $35,000 that Jacek didn't have to worry about, although since Jacek had an animate relationship with his cameras, he was probably going to miss it anyway.

'She is the best there is,' Jacek said, meaning Etta, and Charlie nodded, not saying anything when Jacek added that she had told him she was going to take a few weeks off.

The doctor drove into the yard in a late model four-wheel drive. He had a shiny bald head and brought the cold and the snow into the house with him. He and Jacek and Magda spoke Polish as he unwrapped Charlie's dressings on the kitchen table, like a bloody package of fish. Charlie sat mutely through it all, having his temperature taken, while they spoke about him, and antibiotics were taken out of the briefcase and left on the table. He looked down at his naked, swollen and red hands and listened to the sound of their voices and felt tired and confused. The doctor had a vodka, and Magda and Jacek had one too, and when Charlie's turn came, they gave him a glass of water and three separate pills to take instead. 'But I want a drink,' Charlie said, to which Magda replied, with the doctor nodding his assent, that if he didn't do exactly what he was told he would be in the burns unit for a month and might lose his hands.

Charlie knew this couldn't be true, but it was discouraging nonetheless. Before he could muster any resistance, they had him upstairs in bed, and to Charlie's surprise, the doctor had taken an IV drip out of his case. 'Is that for me?' 'Who else?' Jacek said as the doctor bade him bare his arm to introduce the drip line. So he was sick, Charlie thought, sick enough to stay here for ever. It seemed like a dispensation, and as Charlie fell asleep, under the cold canopy of snow over the skylight, he felt that he might never return to his old life again.

He woke the next morning to the bright stab of late morning sun, knowing he had dreamed of the woman on fire. Nothing definite in the way of an image, just the physical sense of her holding on to him, a strange feeling, full of desire, at her pressing her body against his and the flame leaping between them. With the difference that none of it had hurt, and as they fell together, he had felt her breasts against his chest. It was strange to be lying on a bed so far away wanting someone and wishing he could whisper her name.

He could smell coffee downstairs, so he sat up and pulled out his IV line. He tried to put on his trousers, but he couldn't do up his buttons. So he went downstairs with one of Jacek's dressing gowns held closed around himself with his elbows. Magda was working at the kitchen table with a manuscript and a dictionary, and when she saw him she got up and tied the dressing gown cord around his waist and generally straightened him up. He felt unshaven and a mess and tried to turn away when she was close so she wouldn't have to smell his breath. This was getting ridiculous, he thought, but when he went to the coffee on the stove, he couldn't pour or lift or do anything. He turned and looked at her and shrugged and she came and put a cup to his lips and wiped away a drip on his chin, when he had finished. 'Back to bed,' she said, and he did as he was told. He even put back his IV line, feeling subdued and obedient.

He was like that for a week, and the two of them took turns feeding him and he kept apologising and feeling pathetic and unable to focus. The doctor came, and the medications were changed, and there were new fancy burn dressings with bright shining foil, and he slept and woke and watched the flow of the drip and the sun and clouds crossing the skylight above his head. 'I should be in hospital,' he said to Jacek. 'You are. Turn over,' and he swabbed down Charlie's back with a sponge. 'I can tell,' Jacek added. 'You cannot stand this much longer.'

'I keep dreaming about her,' Charlie said.

Jacek was in the bathroom next door, emptying the basin of water and squeezing out the sponge. He said nothing.

'Maybe we should stop doing this,' Charlie ventured. 'The road trips.'

'Magda agrees with you.'

'And you?'

Jacek came back and sat down on the edge of Charlie's bed.

'We do this thing together. You are good. I am good. Someone else will do it worse.'

'Why do it at all?'

Neither said anything. They knew why they did it, but it seemed ridiculous to rehearse the reasons or to evaluate them now that everything had gone wrong and someone had died because of it. You either kept on or you stopped, and neither knew what they would do now. The honest truth was that it didn't depend on what they said or thought, but on how they would feel, much later, when the assignments were offered, when they watched a situation develop somewhere and felt that desire again, to be there, to be in the middle of it and to be working together.

They knew what the mistake had been: to trust Benny, whom Charlie had instinctively recognised as a chancer. It always came down to this sort of judgement of a stranger: would he deliver? would he betray? did he have any capacity to improvise if things went into that zone of uncertainty or chaos? Benny had been the mistake, but what kind of mistake was that? The kind nothing can stop you making, and which you would make again. They'd tried to save her; they'd intended none of this; they weren't responsible for the war; they had been doing their job. End of story.

Except that it wasn't. Or wouldn't be. Or couldn't be.

'What's Magda say?'

'That it's too high a price to pay in order just to feel that you are alive.'

It was dark now, and the light on Jacek's face was from the single reading lamp. He was bent over, leaning both palms on his knees, looking nowhere in particular, long thin pale hair falling forward and obscuring half his face. He looked the way he always did, tired and distant, with the possibility of very rapid movement just a second away. But it occurred to Charlie that in all the time they had worked together, he had never asked himself whether Jacek could go on, never wondered whether his friend was feeling the same hollowed-out, desolate feeling inside. For it had been Magda who had made Charlie feel that Jacek must be immune to this desolation. It was strange to think that maybe there was no protection at all against this feeling, not even a woman who would do anything for you.

'Your wife called again,' Jacek said. 'Every day in fact.'

Charlie said nothing. Men, in Charlie's experience, did not talk about their wives to other men. Not really. Things were said, but nothing that went close. All Charlie knew, for example, was what Magda did and that they had been together ever since Jacek got out of jail for the trick with the garbage can. He had never told Jacek the least thing about Elizabeth, flautist, music teacher, now deputy school principal. It all just seemed irrelevant, an intrusion on the best thing about their relationship, which was that they were hunters together.

Down in the valley hadn't been the only time Jacek had saved his life. There had been Karte Seh hospital in Kabul, when Hekmatyar's incoming was reducing every adobe wall they sheltered behind to dust. Jacek pulled him away and got them into the Jeep and back to the Intercontinental when Charlie would have pushed them into catching a round or worse. And Charlie had returned the compliment in Huambo, when Jacek stepped around the compound wall to film the boy with the scar on his cheek, coming up the street towards them, Rambo on weed, firing and dancing, weapon on his hip, spraying bullets to and fro, hopping and popping on the balls of his feet. He was shooting up the street the way a kid back home would play with a water hose, but it was Jacek's call – that by turning over just then, the boy wouldn't play the gun on them. Because the kid knew, hey, this is show-time. I'm on TV. The whole world's going to see me dance. And so it proved. He just went right past, jiving and jumping, as Jacek turned and pulled the focus tight on the kid's dilated, bloodshot eyes. Great images. They'd won an award at some film festival. Jacek was concentrating so hard he didn't see

53

the sniper in the charred upstairs window across the street. The first bullet dropped the kid, and the second one would have dropped Jacek, but Charlie got to him first and yanked him back behind the wall.

So this was what bound them together, faith in each other's animal instincts. And it got so that they didn't trust anybody else, or at least Charlie didn't. But he could see that Jacek had always trusted Magda, and that she was one of the sources of sound judgement, no matter how far away they were from each other. Every night Jacek would stroll away from the camp or the bivouac or the compound or the hotel and Charlie would see him on his cellphone talking to her. Charlie had no such resource at home, and he never called when he was out on the road. Well, he had called a couple of times, but the distances were just too great to bridge, him in some fucked-up dive and her and Annie in the kitchen, standing by the fridge with the magnets holding the school schedule and the photo of the three of them in the Rockies. The lines were bad, and when Elizabeth said, don't do this again, he hadn't really disagreed. But that was why he wasn't going home. Not yet, anyway.

He had been in love, Charlie knew, and there were photographs to prove it: Elizabeth in the Italian summer dress with the buttons that undid to reveal that she was wearing nothing underneath; her looking across the table in the restaurant in Volterra as if there was nobody there but him.

He no longer believed his own memory, but he could see what it was like from the photographs. There actually was a shot of that half-kilo bag of cherries, soaked with juice, beginning to disintegrate, on the white sheet of that hotel bedroom in the half-light. The ones they had fed each other, smeared on each other, shutters closed, naked and wet at the very beginning of it all. Those cherries and the purple stain they made on her skin. And the cold-eyed photograph taken before. What kind of idiot takes a photograph of something like that, when he has a woman in a hotel room on a summer afternoon? What's the curatorial impulse? Or worse, what accounts for the sense, from the very beginning, that one day it will be over and he will need proof that it ever took place at all?

He had never thought that he would lose all of this, that it would seem ruined by what had happened after. Weren't some things supposed to be safe from ruin? Like being in love for the first time, in a foreign hotel, on a summer afternoon? Wasn't that supposed to remain untrammelled, no matter how badly everything turned out? Weren't you entitled to remember something like that together, and just feel glad, in your separate ways, that it had been possible? He had no idea how she remembered it, only he was sure it wasn't the way he did.

Come to think of it, what did he and Annie remember in common? He could be out there, in some fly-blown billet at night and count through the time change in order to imagine where his daughter might be at that very hour: on the bus home, with her satchel, or coming through the door for a snack, or lying in bed looking up at the Day-Glo stars she'd patched there to watch their fading when the lights were turned out. No, it wasn't about love, it was about what they had in common. Charlie sat there, Jacek's weight on the end of the bed, and wondered why it was that when he said to Annie, 'Don't you remember?' she so often didn't. Sometimes it was because she had been too young, sometimes because what she remembered was altogether out of his field of vision, like the time they had made that sunny afternoon climb up the switchbacks of Mount Assiniboine, half of it with her on his back. She didn't remember the top, the view that made you want to cue 'Ode to Joy' at about 1,000 decibels, and she didn't remember being carried or how good it felt to be together. Her one memory, she said, had been of that squirrel stealing a nut from her pack during the picnic. What picnic? What squirrel? He'd been sitting beside her and he never even saw it. Charlie knew that it was stupid to fret about this kind of thing, but he couldn't help it. The whole point of a family was encapsulated in 'Do you remember that time when?' In the good old days, he could do that with his own parents. Frank and Mika always gamely joined in, adding embroidery of their own to the tapestry of recollection they made together, though now he had to wonder whether they were humouring him, their one and only. Charlie, thinking like a father now, asked himself what common family memory actually was, what it was that they had been creating together all those years, he, Elizabeth and Annie.

The good thing about Jacek was that you could sit in silence for long periods of time, each of you thinking these kinds of thoughts.

'You'll have to go home,' Jacek said.

'I'm not ready,' Charlie replied.

'She sounds bad,' Jacek observed, noncommittally. It was never his style to tell Charlie what to do. But it was clear that he thought Charlie's habit of endless deferral was beginning to catch up with him.

'She's fine,' Charlie said, and he meant it. Whatever else was true, Elizabeth would be fine without him.

Magda brought up some soup on a tray. Jacek pulled

up a chair and they were going to feed him, but Charlie said he wanted to do it himself. So he tried. The soup didn't always get down his throat, but it felt good to be trying. They sat and watched him.

'What's your secret?' he said finally, looking at them both, the way they sat there, so companionably together.

'He is away a lot,' Magda said and smiled. 'And we are two hours from the city,' Jacek added, pleased that his wife was not going to tell Charlie anything. Jacek went out and came back with a bottle of Wyborowa. 'To hell with the doctor,' he said, and they passed it around. Charlie liked the way she drank, looking at him as it went down.

He stayed for another four days. He got better and was able to do up his buttons and dress himself and go downstairs, past Magda, working at the kitchen table, out into the yard, feeling the cold run through him. He spent hours in Jacek's workshop, watching him take an old camera apart and clean it, piece by piece, with a set of fine brushes and a jet air blower that made a sharp dry hiss. The paraffin heater between them made them drowsy, and so did the work. Charlie just watched, and Jacek would hold a piece up to the light and clean it and assemble all the pieces on a white linen cloth. He took two cameras apart down to their optics, and then assembled them again. It was quiet in the workshop, and sometimes Jacek wouldn't talk for an hour at a time, and Charlie would sit there and feel the silence as a kind of monastery where he was safe from harm.

Twice a day, they went out and fed the pigs, although Charlie couldn't carry the feed pails so he mostly sluiced out the shit with a hose and leaned over the pens and watched the big ones grunt and feed and the little ones nuzzle and suck. Jacek said that in his experience pigs were the least disappointing creatures he had ever known. They made him a little money too, and when Magda pulled the big ham off the larder beam and cut Charlie a slice, he thought this was the life. Except, of course, that it wasn't. It was theirs.

They had meals in the evenings, and Charlie ran the root vegetables through the colander for Magda, and stood close by her at the sink, and they talked about the book she was copy-editing for a publisher in Hamburg. They listened to gloomy orchestral music from Polish composers – Penderecki, Gorecki, Szymanowski, Magda explained – sitting in silence in the television room, Jacek in the chair by the window, Magda with her bare feet curled up beneath her in a chair on the opposite side of the room, and Charlie lying on the couch, staring upwards and wondering whether music had colour, and what mixture of cobalt, blue and black this music was.

His wife stopped calling, and Etta didn't ring either and he felt that he was at peace, except for the recurring dream of the woman on fire and her embrace. It was as if a moment in time was going to take an eternity to disclose itself, the pressure of her fingers on his shoulder-blades, the force of her cheek against his, the incredible smell of her singed hair, all of it recurring over and over as if struggling still to make its meaning plain.

He talked about the woman with Magda, trying to find a way to describe this terrible feeling of intimacy with a total stranger, how they were locked together in an embrace which had ended with death. What was difficult to find words for was the sense that it had all been a mistake, a joke, a dare between men, with these unbearable consequences for someone whose name he didn't even know. Magda listened – as she must be listening to Jacek telling the same story at night, while she lay by his side in their bedroom – and after a while Charlie realised that it must be puzzling for her that he seemed to expect her to know what it all meant. For she didn't know: she merely seemed to think of the woman as the symbol of all the other people in mortal harm who had impinged upon her husband's life and found their way, momentarily, between the cross-hairs of his lens. She felt compassion for them, but in an abstract kind of way, while for Charlie this woman was no symbol at all. She had been so terribly real that he could not get the smell of her burning flesh out of his memory.

'You won't always dream about her, Charlie,' was what Magda said, which Charlie knew was true, but not very comforting. If he stopped dreaming about her, Charlie said, he would betray her. If he continued to dream about her, his life would become impossible.

'What does betrayal have to do with it?' Magda wanted to know, looking up from her manuscript as Charlie walked about her kitchen, sufficiently recovered now to hold the vodka bottle in his hand.

'Because we're the ones who know what she went through. So if we forget, it just seems even more point-less than it already is.'

'So who makes us Mr Memory?' Jacek wanted to know from the other side of the room.

Charlie laughed. Mr Memory was the best thing in Hitchcock's *Thirty-Nine Steps*, the vaudeville guy with the pencil moustache and a perfect memory, hired by the bad guys to memorise the secret code. It was all a bit far-fetched, but the final scene was great when

Mr Memory was on stage in the vaudeville house and Hannay stood up in the smoky audience and asked him to repeat the secret formula, and before the bad guys could stop him, Mr Memory began spilling it out, right there on stage. What was poignant was the look in his eyes, as if he was truly helpless in the face of knowledge and the obligation to disclose it. Standing there on stage, with his wax moustache and bow-tie, transfixed by the obligation to speak, he couldn't help reeling off the secret formula until a bullet from his controller, fired from the wings, put him out of his misery.

'Nobody makes us Mr Memory,' Charlie said. 'We do it to ourselves.'

He got Jacek to drive him to the airport the next day. Outside the house, he held Magda tightly between his still-bandaged hands and as he got into the car he felt that he had done well to restrain more effusive displays. Actually, he had been pretty effusive. What he said to her, very close, was that she had been good to a stranger, and she replied that he had never been a stranger. With that, she kissed him, a little peck right on his lips, and he got into the car feeling happy.

The road was bare and dry between ploughed fields and Jacek said almost nothing till they were at the airport. 'So we go out again or what?' he asked when the car was at the ramp in front of departures.

'I want to go to Belgrade,' Charlie said.

'And kill that son of a bitch?' Jacek said with his usual wry lack of affect, opening the door of the Lada and giving Charlie a gentle push to help him up. It was one of Jacek's better moves, Charlie thought later as the plane lifted off for London, giving words to a thought that had been in both of their minds, just beneath the level of awareness, from the second they had seen that lighter applied to the hem of that dress.

Yes, kill that son of a bitch.

Six

When he got to his front door, he opened it with his key and stood in the hall and put his bag down. He went into the sitting room on the left with the floor to ceiling bookshelves the length of the far wall. He could see the rows of Mika's books, the ones with the Russian titles on the spines that he hadn't the heart to throw away when he cleared out the house in Dedham and that he kept promising himself he'd learn how to read one day. There were Frank's too, one row above, the stout-hearted memoirs of battle, and a couple of ones – *Home Carpenters' Almanac*, for example – that Charlie had salvaged from the garage. By the television stood the rows of Charlie's video tapes and next to the stereo system his blues and country and western: fifteen separate Johnny Cash. 'I shot a man in Reno,' Charlie said to himself, 'just to watch him die.'

In the middle of the room, placed so that it faced the bay window and had a good view of the street, was the music stand and Elizabeth's flute. He could see she was still working on the Haydn, because the music was on the stand. He'd been away for a month.

'Charlie?' She was on the top step of the landing

looking down at him standing in the hall. He nodded and she came down slowly, drying her hands on her apron. She was wearing the black dress, and her hair was up. She had the long silver earrings on that brought out the fine shape of her neck.

'You going to a party?' he asked.

'Rae and Barbara are coming over. I'm cooking. Life goes on Charlie,' she said, reaching the bottom step.

'Where's Annie?'

'At the Duggans. On a sleep-over.'

He followed her through the living room into the kitchen at the back. The table, by the sliding door out into the garden, was set for three. He watched as she set a fourth place.

'Why the beard?' she asked, and he said that he hadn't been able to hold a razor, but now he could and later he would go upstairs and get rid of it.

He went over to the cupboard, took out the single malt he knew was there and got a glass, then corrected himself, took out two and sat down at the table, still in his coat, and tried to get the cork out of the bottle. She watched him and came over and took it out of his hands and poured two inches for him.

'You too,' he said and she did as he asked. She drank the whisky, with a grimace, straight down, but she didn't sit with him. She went back to her cooking, and he sat there watching her back. She had good legs, like her mother, firm calves and a nice taper down to the ankle.

'You can't get away with not talking,' she said over her shoulder. 'You did that before and you can't do it this time.' She was right, of course. He did have a habit of shutting everything down when he didn't know what to think or feel. He would just go mute and there had been times in their marriage when it went on for days, for example at the end of that thing with whatever her name was. Re-entry was always hell. He felt like a diver, having to come up slowly, fifteen feet at a time, with the wobbly blue sky so far away above him and never getting any closer. The best way was just to take it easy, letting the surroundings go to work on you. He sat by the table and looked about him, remembering when the wall had stopped there and they had knocked it through to make the kitchen bigger. The history of the room, and the house in which it stood, was reeling him in, and so were the cooking smells on the stove. She was doing that thing with chicken and vegetables that started on the burners and ended up in the oven and came out tasting of paprika and pepper.

He should stay: his father had, his mother had. Look where it got them. No really, look where it got them, faithful to the end, Mika holding Frank's head in her arms on the garage floor, saying Russian prayers over him. Or so she said. He hadn't been there. He had been here. In this house when his dad died, an ocean away, in theirs. He drank, cupping the glass with two bandaged hands and looked at her and knew he had to say something.

'If the office hadn't phoned,' she said.

'I just couldn't.'

'Don't do this to us.'

'I'm not doing anything.'

She let that pass. 'What happened?' It wasn't that she didn't know. She must have made ten calls to Jacek and Magda. She would have had the gist from them and from the office. But she wanted to hear it from him. He owed it to her.

'We got caught in an ambush and a girl got killed.'

'I saw the footage, Charlie. She was burning.' She had her back to the stove and she was vehement and angry, because it made her sick to think he was fobbing her off. But it was all that he could get out of his throat. He was trying to understand why it was that when you told a story, once, for good – in this case to Etta – it all dried up inside you when you were ordered to tell it again.

'Come on, Charlie. Tell me.' She never begged.

'I got burned. I was trying to put her out.'

'Oh Charlie, Jesus Christ, if only you'd rung us,' she said, in a voice full of pain for him, and for them. He could tell she was doing the best she could. She was trying. He could tell from the catch in her voice.

'I know.'

'You need to see a doctor.' She stayed with her back to the kitchen surfaces, but her hands made a gesture towards him.

'My hands are fine. Really. Want to see?'

'I don't mean your hands.'

It cut him to hear her say that. She was the one he had the history with, and whatever else was wrong, she knew him well.

'I don't need a doctor.'

She shook her head and bent so that her hair came down over her face, as if she wanted to hide from the sight of him for a moment. Then she straightened, turned her back and steadied a lemon on the chopping board to slice it.

'They got burned. But they're fine.'

She began stirring something in a cup. She was making salad dressing. He could smell the lemon. 'Why Jacek rather than me?' Her back stayed turned.

'Don't know.'

He really didn't, now that he was here. He could say Jacek had been through it all with him and she hadn't. He could say, though she would have thrown the salad dressing at him, that it was a guy thing, needing the comfort of a man, although that was actually part of the truth. Nothing was clear now, because he could see all that he had spurned by not coming home and how much of him was here between these four walls. Everything was rooting him to the spot and taking away the power of speech. There was the fact that he knew the name of the village in northern Italy, and could even see that tiny, neat as a pin shop where he had stood outside, too big and clumsy to be allowed in, while she sat inside buying the glasses that she had put by every place on the table where he was nursing his drink. He knew why she set a table like this, when it was only for Barbara and Rae, two friends of hers from work, why she dressed up. It was what her mother did. He knew the exact components of her salad dressing – garlic, Dijon, salt, pepper, one part lemon to two parts olive oil – because it was her dad's recipe. The weight of all these facts crushed down on his chest. But he said nothing and she just shook her head again and gave the lemon a hard squeeze.

He knew he ought to be taking control of the situation and steering them both in the right direction. He knew what that direction was too – it should all end with him putting out his hand and saying he wanted to go to bed, and she would take it and help him off with his coat and take him upstairs. And then he would throw his clothes on the chair and lie down in the bed and she would come and they would lie side by side and after much effort of will he would reach over and put his arm around her and with more effort of will he would say he was sorry for not having been able to phone or give her any indication of where he had been. He could see the right path all right.

'Go upstairs and shave,' she said. 'They'll be here in ten minutes.'

He did as he was told, finding his shaving things put away beneath the sink, and their place taken on the shelf below the mirror by her cleansers and pads. He lathered himself up, averting his eyes from the eyes that met him in the mirror, and cut himself a few times.

When he looked, she was leaning against the door-frame, watching how his old face came up clean as the razor peeled away the whiskers. He just kept on going, watching her out of the corner of his eye, when he went on to treat his cuts with the styptic pencil.

He spoke her name to the mirror. 'Elizabeth.' Liz Drew as was. Eldest daughter of Bart and Carla Drew of Norwood, Massachusetts. 'You're kidding,' she said, and her face lit up, when they met for the first time at a party in London and he told her that he was from Dedham, just up Route 1A. After all these years, she was still the girl most likely to succeed. Age had not dimmed her. She was still smiling out of her graduation picture. Not now, of course, but she could. He felt, in an absurd way, that it was to his credit that he hadn't destroyed that in her.

He could see Bart in that thick cardigan Carla knitted for him against the icy night air, sauntering down at Charlie's side to the liquor store at the bottom of their road. They came back with enough stuff, as Bart put it happily, to launch a rocket to Mars, and they drank all of it. That was how Christmas should be, Carla said, when it was all over and he was on the floor beside her, picking that tree decoration stuff, the silver thread, out of the plush pile of her carpet.

'Charlie.' He could hear Elizabeth whisper his name in the dark woods behind her parents' house, when they were side by side on the path amid the feathery snow, the year they got married.

'Yes,' she said. 'Tell me,' not there, not twenty-four, wrapped in a scarf against the cold, but here and forty-six, with her hair up and her earrings catching the light from the hall.

'I don't know about this thing with Rae and Barbara,' he said.

She had the wry look on her face. 'My war correspondent husband,' she began, 'the guy who gets shot at for a living and he can't hack dinner with Rae and Barbara. No kidding.' She was trying to work one of the better routines from the happy time, her line in comic scorn. It had actually been a bond. He was the useless one, she the one with the comic scorn. It had worked for years and years, and in deference to this, he managed a smile and followed her downstairs to dinner.

It was hell all right. Rae and Barbara couldn't leave it alone. They had seen the footage and they wanted to hear it all first hand, and he had to do his party trick, and he thought that if he had been hoping to regain some credit for good behaviour, he deserved some in the circumstances. But Elizabeth wasn't handing out any medals.

'Poor soul,' Barbara said when he got to the part about how the burned woman went through the flanged plastic doors in the field hospital and didn't come back. What was truly interesting, he thought, was how quickly the silence after that was filled with talk, how they went on to other things, as if he had said something embarrassing but unimportant. Elizabeth listened to him, angry no doubt that Rae and Barbara had got more out of him than she had. She stared at him across the glassware, her hand along the fine line of her jaw, her elbow resting on the table. Afterwards, as their talk eddied around how terrible the world was and how violent, and how did he do what he did, she let him twist in the wind for a while, he could tell, before she got up and cleared the dishes and then threw him an unexpected lifeline, by changing the subject. This left him free to sit there and drink that old red he had bought some time ago and listen to them talk about school.

He could tell that Rae and Barbara knew they had walked into bad marital weather, but they were the good kind of people who just ploughed their earnest conversational furrow, believing feigned obliviousness would help a couple through a bad patch. He stayed silent and watched them talk. He had time to look over at Elizabeth, to look at her as if he was just a guest and could get up at the end of the night and never see her again. He reflected that it was good that she knew who she was and that she had never based her life on assumptions that weren't true. For example, after coming to London to study, she had known she would never make an orchestra, and had gone into teaching, and having done that, she realised she was a better administrator and had become deputy head, an American no less, with an even stronger mid-Atlantic accent than his now, of the school where Rae and Barbara were teaching. Rae taught maths and Barbara chemistry, and Elizabeth was their boss. She liked her job, and they liked her, and Charlie looked on and took it all in, as if he was just passing through.

Christ, they were great people, really, but they took the Lord's time to go. Afterwards Charlie and Elizabeth did the dishes, because the dishwasher was acting up, and she handed him plastic gloves to protect his hands, and he was able to pat the big pots and plates with the towel and put them away on the shelves. They didn't exchange a word, and it ought to have been a companionable silence. But it was not. When he put down the dishtowel and walked through the sitting room and out into the hall, he saw his bag still lying there on the floor. He picked it up and walked to the door. She followed him out into the hall.

'Where the hell are you going?' she demanded. She grabbed him and turned him around. She was shaking him. Then she punched him hard in the chest and knocked him back against the wall.

'What are you doing? Talk to me. You have to.'

But he couldn't, and he couldn't explain why. He shook himself loose and just said Sorry. She shouted his name, but it made no difference. He opened the door and stepped out into the night.

Charlie spent his first of many nights in the railway station hotel. He could afford better, but his view was that he didn't deserve better. He lay in the dark and went to sleep to the sound of someone taking hoarse, fierce pleasure in the room next door.

SEVEN

He woke at first light, still in his clothes, listening to the waking roar of the city through dirty curtains. The bag he had packed in Magda and Jacek's house lay unopened on the floor. He sat up and felt around for his shoes. He had woken up before in a strange hotel room, thinking he had done the irrevocable, only to discover, in time, that he hadn't. But this felt different: as if this was the moment, the pivot on which his life turned.

He imagined Elizabeth standing in the kitchen in the half-light, unable to sleep and Annie, at the Duggans, wrapped in her sleeping-bag on the floor of some kid's room. His own recklessness frightened him. 'Live in truth,' he heard a voice inside him say. What the hell did *that* mean?

He shaved though he didn't want to, because he thought he ought not start out by letting himself go. He changed his clothes, straightened himself up, and then stood there, ready for the day, looking at himself in the mirror. 'Live in truth': what was the truth of this face? He could see his mother and his father, old Mika and Frank, the tender nemesis of all his attempts to be different from them, but the traces of their features were all that was familiar in the visage in the yellow light of the plastic bathroom suite. It felt crazy to look at yourself and think: I'm a middle-aged guy in a hotel bathroom, Mika and Frank's kid, and I've left my family, and I don't have any idea about what happens next.

'Live in truth.'

He had a longing to be right with the world, to be at home in his skin, or whatever the phrase was. He had once thought he knew what it felt like, but he didn't know now and he hadn't known since the woman had died and Etta had left him. He came down the stairs in the hotel, imagining Etta intently, like a voyeur concealed behind a half-open door, watching as she opened her dressing gown and enfolded him in. He watched the scene, like a lonely outsider, but at the same time he could feel his burning palms resting on her shoulders, the moist smell and the warmth of her body. He felt less homeless to think that she was out there in the same city, but to tell the truth, he did not know where she was.

In the hotel lobby, he stopped and stood reliving their last moment together, in front of the church. He could now see how he must have looked, waving his bandaged hands about, pretending he knew what he was doing, when he was actually sick and completely out of control. He almost laughed. It took a weird kind of talent for self-destruction to shoot yourself in the foot like that.

The first thing to do was to fix what had gone wrong. He was a believer in the new day. It was an expression of his father's. According to Frank, when you got lost in life, you had to retrace your steps and start over. You had to keep believing you could find a life that made sense. It was about the only advice Frank had ever given him, in the shy, indirect way he had, standing at the work-bench in the garage, in between the noise from his drills, and so low Charlie wasn't sure he'd heard it. 'Find the new day.' Charlie had to find it now.

He phoned Etta's extension from the pay phone in the hotel lobby. He heard the answerphone reply, in a cool voice, that she would be out of the office for three weeks. Next he tried her cellphone. As unit manager, she gave it out to all the crews on the road. It was standard procedure, only now, when it answered, her voice instructed callers to reach Megan instead.

He didn't know where else to look. He had been to Etta's apartment once, about five years ago, to pick up some tickets on the way to the airport, but he'd never find it now, and she might have moved in between. She hadn't let him in the door, just smiled and handed him the tickets. He could hear some classical piano music playing in the background. She had looked young, her hair braided back at the nape of her neck, wearing a blue dress, her feet bare with red toenails and she looked perfectly happy and self-sufficient on her own. No closer, Charlie, had been her message then, and he had taken it in good grace, giving her a little wave as he stepped back into the taxi.

He walked out into the square in front of the railway station and seemed to have eyes only for everything that was vile: the spit on the sidewalk and the vomited food in a starburst by the subway entrance and the bloody gash on a drunken beggar's forehead. Life's redeeming features must still be around here somewhere, he thought, but he couldn't see them, and as he was swept into the people funnelling down into the subway, he felt he was on his way down into hell.

The subway car was packed, and they got stuck

between stations, and he was hemmed in, with his eyes shut. Then he remembered a story Etta had told him that night in the Esplanade about Jimmy something, the singer who was a star in her country. She said he looked like that Australian, with the same ringlet hairstyle, and he sang songs about love, in a four-octave range, and the people thought he was the greatest thing there was. They even crowned him the King on one of their TV shows, and when he put the crown on his head, Etta said, he looked as if he really was the King. She began to laugh, and so had he, as they lay on the bed together while she described the sequinned suits he wore, and the sweat pouring down his face as the girls clawed at him from the front row of the stalls. The great part of her story was how Jimmy had woken early one morning, disturbed by a cock crowing in his neighbour's field. He grabbed the gun he kept on the bedside table. He began firing it – and this was the point – from *inside* the bedroom, shattering the windows, while his wife sat up in bed begging him to stop. He just went higher and higher, waving the gun around his head shouting that nobody had the right to disturb King Jimmy. Then the gun went off again, and Jimmy slipped down with a stunned look and when his wife got to him on the floor, he was staring up at her with a neat small hole in the side of his head.

Charlie remembered how Etta laughed, with her hand to her mouth and a look just short of tears when she described Jimmy's fate. She had sympathy for Jimmy, who had seemed to understand, but just a little too late, that life could get completely out of control. Charlie was thinking about Etta so hard he was surprised when the train lurched into his station and he was bundled out on to the platform.

She wasn't in her office, of course, but he lingered by the glass door observing the neatness of her cubicle, so unlike the others, the desk swept clean, and the files with their tabs in order in the tray and her handwriting on each of them. He hadn't noticed before how the chaos of the newsroom, all those piles of newspaper, discarded scripts, dusty monitors, Post-Its, half-empty cups of coffee, seemed to stop at her doorway and give way to her serene space. Looking at her monitor and its mouse, the filing cabinet sealed shut, the way she kept the disorder at bay, he wished he had paid attention to it all before this moment. She had left a pair of black high heels by the coat-rack. He wanted to pick them up, run his hands along the inside of the leather, feel for the indentation of her toes in the sole, but when he tried the door, it was locked.

There was no one in yet, except the cleaners, and he sat in his coat in front of his desk, looking at the mess as if it belonged to someone else. He poked around in the newspapers now weeks old and that script idea he had and then he swept it all into the bin and held it out for the cleaner in the sari, with a blood spot in the middle of her forehead, who took it without a word and dumped it into a black plastic bag attached to her cart.

He had been a journalist from his early twenties, he thought, in a pompous kind of way like someone about to make a speech or a confession. And at the age of twenty-four, when he was a buck private, he managed to parlay his high school sports writing into a berth on the *Stars and Stripes* at Danang. He never did see combat, like his dad, but he saw what combat had done to the people brought to the base hospital. All he remembered was going down the wards, talking to guys who had left parts of themselves up there on Route 9 or Khe Sanh, and how, when he was by their bedsides, writing up their story in his notebook, he would look up into their eyes and see something there that made him feel ashamed of himself without knowing why, though he knew now. He filed some stories, lies all of them, about how brave everyone was, and came back determined that he would be a little more truthful. After Danang, there had been nearly thirty years of it, from linotype and typewriters to ENG and satellite feeds, from home town papers to the metropolis and from the metropolis to the London bureau. What he had to show for it was an office of his own, where he could shut the door, as well as half a secretary, three awards on his wall, and more experience than he knew what to do with. Not understanding it, he had reduced it all to a set of stories told whenever he was drunk or there was a woman he wanted to impress. The point of these stories was: look at me, how I have lived. But it seemed obvious to him now that he had been left almost completely untouched by his life. Tired of it, perhaps, but untouched, as if it had all been just a very long action movie and no curtain.

Except, of course, the woman on fire. He looked at his hands, lifted off the bandages. They were better now. He pulled the bandages off entirely and threw them in the bin. The new skin was pink and tender. But they were fine. If people didn't shake his hands, he would be OK.

'Where the hell have you been?'

It was Megan, large, cheerful, English, the first in and the last out every night and nobody really knew how she lived. With a dog. With a cat. Who knew? Who cared?

He swivelled around and realised how pleased he was by the sight of her, pink cheeks, hair askew, perennially dishevelled in those capacious print dresses that thankfully concealed her moving parts.

'We've been looking for you,' she said.

'You haven't,' Charlie said, smiling. 'Jacek phoned. So you knew.'

'I mean we did, but you did bloody well disappear.'

'Needed a break, Meg, a bit of peace and quiet.'

'Your wife didn't bloody know.'

'She's very cross with me, I quite agree.' Even though Megan had never cast eyes on Elizabeth, she took the woman's part. It was her trade union.

'You all right?' She had a great south London accent. Awwright? She gave him her quizzical look, the one that registered that he belonged to another tribe, men in trouble with women.

'Just fine, Meg.'

There were footsteps and voices in the corridor. The early shift was coming in for the one o'clock. Dannie. Martin, the Luscious Maria. Foster and Imran.

Hey, they said.

Hey, Charlie said, waving a little wanly.

They weren't really curious about where he'd been. They didn't want to know. They were satisfied with the minimum: that there had been an accident, something about his hands.

'Charles, it was a good story,' Luscious Maria said and turned her molten brown eyes upon him from the doorway. She was the only person on earth who called him Charles. She was a comic figure, Luscious Maria, a serious and melancholy Christian Palestinian whose curves and skin and dark eyes attracted men with outsize wrist-watches, chest hair and big money in import-export, when what she wanted, as she once confessed to Charlie on their solo late night drink together, was a

77

man with sensitivity. To which Charlie had replied that there was no such thing, not really, as a man with sensitivity.

'Thanks, Maria,' he said. But he wasn't thinking about her.

'Meg, could I have the tape? All the output.'

He hadn't seen the pictures and now there was nothing else that mattered. Meg came back in a minute with two cassettes, one the finished story, the other Jacek's output tape. She said that Shandler wanted to see him at ten, but although Charlie took this in and registered that it meant trouble, he was already putting the tape in the deck. Meg wanted to watch too, but he shooed her out and sat there alone, blinds down, seeing it all over again.

The version was cut to the standard 90 seconds and had run, so he could see from the tab, on the 1 and the 6 a month or so before. They had kept his stand-up in the dug-out, though it was terrible, since he looked as jarred and scared as the three camouflaged village boys just behind him in the shot. The rest of the voice-over was by the seedy Stedman, whose voice blessed every event – from earthquakes to celebrity weddings – with the same empty portentousness. 'Militia units seen here, in the uniforms of. . . .' It was all the long lens stuff Jacek had shot of the blue armoured vehicle, the commander coming out to the house, the flames rising from the door. And then Jacek's shot went in closer, as the woman came out of the house. You could see the trick with the lighter. The flames on her clothes. Charlie got close to the monitor, moving the dials forward and back, re-running it over and over. Then he pulled out the output tape and scrolled through Jacek's shots, all the drops and edits. There was one shot; – unusable because too fast, too shaky – there goes another award, Charlie thought – of the woman running towards him. If you slowed it right down, until she was jerking frame by frame, you could begin to see in the smoke and the aureole of flame around her the widening hole of her mouth. Opening and closing. Opening and closing.

Charlie played with the dials, back and forward, but he could never get her face to come into resolution, could never freeze it in such a way that he could print it and have something to hold on to. She slipped away into the flames, and all he could feel was the thud of her body against his and the smell of burning and the groaning from her lips near his ear.

But if you slowed down the militia unit footage, to the moment when the commander got out and came down the path to the house, you could see his face clearly in a frame or two. After she caught and began to flare like a torch, yes, you could see his face. Charlie slowed it down, froze the frame, pressed print and then waited, with a feeling of being satiated and certain of at least one thing, while the single image came off the printer.

He had it in his hand when he came into Shandler's office and he was studying it when Shandler gave him the lecture. It wasn't easy of course, because the footage had run everywhere and the network had recouped every dime. But the thing about Shandler was that he liked to make you think the money didn't matter. There was also the principle, though Charlie never could anticipate what 'the principle' would turn out to be. Charlie got the whole pompous lecture, the one about not being professional, about not telling them, leaving crew behind, taking leave without permission, not seeking appropriate medical help, the whole boring administrative stick. Charlie even had time, so little did

Shandler's words imprint themselves upon him, to observe that their whole relationship was a cliché: Johnson the field man confronts Shandler the desk man. The desk man always wins.

'So what's it going to be?' Charlie said.

'I had considered dismissal,' Shandler said.

'So why don't you?'

'The footage was too good.'

'And it would look ridiculous to fire the man who burned his hands getting it.'

'Something like that.'

'So I'm grounded.'

'Desk assignments for a while. Glad to oblige.' Shandler looked at him over the top of his rimless half-glasses.

'Look at this.' He handed Shandler the picture: a man of about forty, dark hair, trim and tight inside his uniform, one hand outstretched, with the lighter at the end of it.

'So?'

'I want to find him.'

'Not on my dime, Charlie.'

So Charlie said what he had always wanted to say, what he had often rehearsed, but this time it was for real, and he only had one take, so he had to muster years of professional experience into his voice. He gave his boss a long look and said,

'Shandler, you are such an asshole.'

As he turned and walked out, Charlie had the distinct feeling that he had burned every bridge left.

Except one. He left the office, crossed town and made his way to what he thought was the right bus stop. He wasn't absolutely sure, not being the *perfect* father, that she used this one, but it was the one closest to school, so he waited, and sure enough, a little shoal of them in their red and white uniforms showed up, talking so intently as they came along that Annie looked shocked to see him standing there smiling.

'What are you doing here?' she said. The other girls eddied back to give her room to deal with this peculiar creature.

'I've come to take you home.'

'But you never take me home.'

She didn't look like either of them, he thought. The genes had skipped, and there was a fresh-faced version of Mika looking up at him, squinting at him just the way his mother used to.

She added for good measure, 'Mom said you're away.'

'Your Mom's right. I was away and now I'm back for a day and I'm here to take you home.' He said all this brightly, keeping everything light. That was what being a parent was all about, keeping control of the emotional weather.

She still seemed puzzled when the bus came and she stepped on and flashed her pass, and he had to ask what the fare was. The other girls, a trio of them, sat at the back of the bus, whispering and watching them, and she sat on her own, and left a place for him, and he was touched by how hard she was trying, especially with her friends staring at her. He gave the three harpies a cheery wave as he sat down.

He asked what the lessons had been, and she gave a shudder and said music, and it made him laugh to think that the genes had played this second curious trick. Elizabeth had had to reconcile herself to the fact that her own talent wasn't going to have any succession, just as she had been reconciled to only having one, despite her oft-stated conviction that Charlie was the disaster he was because he had been an only child.

Annie pulled her exercise book out of her satchel and sat it on her knees, and he opened it and looked at the procession of her rounded, laborious letters, struggling to catch up with her thoughts. He followed her composition down one side of the page and over on to the next and the one after it. She was in a Gothic phase, and there was a lot of moonlight, and sighing trees, and a dog that howled. He approved of the dog, he said, and suggested that they needed to know what colour it was.

'But it's pitch dark,' she said. 'You can't tell what colour the dog would be.'

'What about the moonlight?' he countered, and she looked at him and conceded that the dog was probably light brown.

The bus let the harpies off, and she was more at home with him then, sitting in silence and then asking where he had been. He had to hand it to Elizabeth: the protection was full time. He just said, 'Away.'

When they got off at her stop he held out his hand and she took it, and all the way up through the park he felt the keen, new sensitivity of his raw skin against hers. 'I'm just going to drop you off,' he said as he rang the doorbell. 'Then I've got to get back to work.'

'But it's almost dark,' she said, disbelievingly. He was stroking her face and giving her a soft shove in the small of her back to get her inside, as the door opened. Elizabeth registered, then concealed, her shock, and shooed Annie inside. 'Be there in a sec, sweetheart,' she said, as Charlie caught a glimpse of Annie looking back at him as the door closed.

'Don't you *ever* do that again,' she hissed.

'Pick my daughter up from school?'

'You fucking well know what I mean,' she said. 'I am keeping up appearances. I do nothing but keep up appearances. Not for your sake. But for hers. And you *will* do what I say.'

'Or?' He wanted to know what kind of threat he was hearing, though he had a fair idea.

'You will never see her again.'

She tried to hit him, but he caught her hand first and held it by the wrist up in the air for a second, then let it fall. She stood back, fighting tears, getting them down so Annie wouldn't see, and then she pushed the door open with her shoulder, turned and went inside, closing it behind her.

EIGHT

Etta flew home to the small town in what Charlie called her little country, and she let herself sink back into the rhythm of her parents' lives. She took her mother shopping and her father to the doctor to have his injections. They were eighty and eighty-four, and they had lived in the same apartment since they were married. She sat with them at night, at the kitchen table, playing cards with her father, while her mother did the dishes. Nothing had changed since her childhood. The lined wallpaper was the same. The fireman's calendar by the door was the same, though a new one came every year. The rituals were the same – reading the local newspaper aloud, while her father nodded and her mother stacked the plates on the draining board. She was glad to be home.

By day, she ironed for her mother and listened to the gossip, noting how the ambit of what she talked about in her small voice had shrunk from the town to the street and from the street to the stairwell of their apartment. Her father was forgetting, but it was the best kind of forgetting, the kind he didn't notice. One night, she stood in the doorway of the room where they slept on separate beds and listened to them breathing slowly through their mouths and she felt that they had become as vulnerable as children.

She paid their bills and made arrangements with their neighbours to get the firewood carried up the three flights and stacked on the balcony. She went for walks on her own, out into the bare fields on the edge of town. One evening, when they were all heading for bed, her mother stroked Etta's face, as they stood in the hallway by the kitchen and said that she looked worried. Care-worn was the actual word. Etta smiled and said she was fine. Her mother said she should go and pay a visit to Uncle Janos. His business was going well and he had moved to a big villa on the heights above town. He still lived alone. Etta kissed her mother on her forehead and told her she should get some rest.

'Why don't you see him? He asks after you.'

'I'm happy for him. It's late, let's go to sleep.'

Her mother went into her bedroom, but as she closed the door she gave her daughter a look, both timid and questioning.

As Etta always did when she came home, she kept away from him. It had long ceased to hurt or even matter very much. She felt nothing, in fact, but she didn't want to run into him and she didn't want to discuss it with her mother, although she wondered what she did or didn't know.

That night, when her parents were asleep, Etta phoned Meg and heard about the scene with Shandler and how it had occurred after Charlie had seen the tapes. Now he had disappeared, nobody knew where. Meg said he had been smiling when he came back down the corridor from Shandler's office and walked straight out holding nothing but a picture. Etta didn't like the sound of this, especially the smile. She'd witnessed his duels with Shandler over the years, and he often behaved stupidly afterwards. The Perrier bottle against the wall, for example. Now he was smiling. Free at last, he would be thinking. Dangerous to think you were free at last, Etta thought, especially if you were Charlie Johnson.

Meg also said that Elizabeth had rung her. She was in a bad state, Meg said, not crying but wanting to know where Charlie was. He had walked out days before, she had checked the usual places and he was nowhere to be found. Elizabeth also asked where Etta was. So Megan had told her that Etta was at her parents', Meg apologised, but Etta said she had done the right thing.

After this call, she rang Poland and Jacek came on, still wide awake, though it was now about one in the morning. She had never met Jacek face to face, but she had booked him countless times. She had heard Charlie's stories, and the gist of them was that Jacek was the more reliable of the pair. Etta certainly thought so. When she told Jacek that Charlie had gone missing, Jacek went silent and then told her what he had said to Charlie as he dropped him off at the airport. Jacek explained that he was sorry he had said it. Or not sorry, because he meant it, but sorry because of where it might lead.

Though, Etta said quickly, it was the clue they needed.

Yes, Jacek agreed. It was a clue.

She left him her number and put the phone down and sat on the end of the bed, rubbing her arms through her nightgown, feeling cold.

Kill the son of a bitch.

The words didn't have to mean exactly what they

said. Charlie exaggerated. He allowed himself to be taken over by rhetoric. He liked the violence of words. He didn't have to mean them. He might just mean he wanted to confront him, yes, confront him, make him feel fear, regret, anything. Not necessarily kill him.

She got out her black book, dialled her numbers and got the information she needed so that when Jacek, who must have been thinking the same, rang and said he was going, she had flights for him too, getting there more or less the same time, or so they hoped. There were visas to be arranged, but if Charlie had got one, so could they, probably at the airport.

Then Magda came on the line and told Jacek to leave them alone. The women hadn't met either but it didn't matter. They both felt as if they had. Magda said she didn't feel easy about these plans, and Etta agreed. Magda said she felt it would be dangerous to unleash Jacek and Charlie together. The event had done Jacek damage too, and he wasn't right and he needed to stay home longer. While she couldn't stop him, there were risks if the two men went out on the road again. Charlie wasn't in any shape either. Etta said she understood. This was when Etta added that she was going too. 'To keep an eye on them,' she said, and they both laughed, the idea being so improbable, but it was what they thought. Neither of them was in the rescue business, and they knew that these were men who couldn't be rescued in any case. But they needed watching. They couldn't be trusted. The words didn't have to mean what they said, but everything could get right out of hand.

Etta told Magda that being a unit manager was all about preparing for consequences, warning crews about them and, occasionally, getting men who didn't know what they were doing to realise that they didn't.

Magda said, 'I want Jacek to come off the road.'

'I don't know how,' Etta replied.

'He needs to see what I see,' Magda said.

'How could they?' Etta replied.

In the morning, she made the calls to Buddy, the fixer Charlie always used in Belgrade and she tipped off Meg, who said she would tell Elizabeth nothing for the moment, except that Jacek was tracking Charlie down. Etta had never met Elizabeth. What had happened was between Charlie and her, and while she had not gone just to nurse him, she had kept hope at bay throughout. When Charlie had wanted her to stick around, she tried to send him back home. So the slate was clean, as far as she was concerned, and she could look Elizabeth in the eye any time. Though she couldn't imagine it would be much fun.

After she kissed her parents goodbye and boarded the plane later that day for London, the problem on her mind was not Elizabeth, but Charlie and Jacek. Something Magda had said the night before stuck in her mind. The two men, Magda said, were in the grip of a bad spell, except that wasn't right, it was more that they were bound together by a new kind of anger she had never seen in Jacek before, and which was – and here Magda searched for the word – *corrupting* him.

Etta hadn't considered this possibility. By *corruption* Magda meant that two men, more or less decent, had been coarsened by the scenes their profession paid them to witness. Neither man would have known what was happening to them, but anyone who cared to look could see the irritable edginess, the distance, the sudden fury that would take them over, for nothing, when they were uncorking a bottle that wouldn't release its cork or the car wouldn't start or . . . anything. Something was taking them over, eroding their capacity to protect themselves from what they saw. Whatever it was, it was eating away at their very judgement. Magda said, you couldn't merely watch what Jacek had seen. You couldn't merely frame it up in the viewfinder, year after year. Etta had seen the footage too and most of the time she didn't even notice it, but now she understood what Magda was trying to say. Those boys with guns, hopping and popping on the balls of their feet, wasting everything with arcs of fire, those chopped and desecrated bodies, those eyes of weeping women, those forlorn barefoot orphans, they slowly came inside and took possession. And once inside, they would never leave. So that when Charlie and Jacek finally saw something that broke their hearts, when they saw the woman die, looking up at them from the realm beyond hope, the only purification would lie through violence.

Etta understood now what Charlie must have been thinking when he walked out of Shandler's office, with the picture of that militia officer in his hand. He would have thought he was free. He would have thought he was in the grip of truth. He would have thought righteousness was within his grasp. But in reality, all the truth and righteousness calling to him was nothing more than annihilation.

Etta saw him so clearly now, with a tenderness made possible by Magda's feeling for her husband. Charlie was not himself and she had to get him to see that.

Kill the son of a bitch.

She wanted him to realise that he owed the woman something better than vengeance. We will not forget you. We will seek justice for you.

As she watched the city emerge out of the dark and the undercarriage groaned loose and the plane began to settle towards the ground, she knew that her chance of getting Charlie to understand any of this was small. At most she might be able to deflect or delay him till she could make him see that he was possessed, not himself. He might hear something in her voice, she reasoned, that would make him pause and consider before taking an irrevocable step. He'd needed her once. He might listen to her now.

NINE

Charlie went to the Moskva on automatic pilot, straight from the airport, the way he always did. Now that he had been suspended the trip was on him, but he thought he needed the Moskva, even though it didn't come cheap. He wanted it to feel like old times. Big handsome Goran behind the desk obliged. 'Like old times,' he said, and smiled as he handed Charlie the key. Goran had always been a minor puzzle. He was so well dressed, and there wasn't a woman who didn't think he was interesting. But he was the night clerk at the Moskva. This suggested either that he possessed an aristocratic soul and didn't care about money or that he was moonlighting for the authorities. As he signed in, under Goran's benevolent gaze, Charlie grew certain that the gorillas would soon know where he was staying. But they probably knew he was there already. That charming creature in the embassy in London who doled out the visas had made certain of that. So what if they knew? They'd let him in, that was all that mattered.

It was reassuring to return to the eccentric double-decker rooms, with their internal balconies and 1930s parquet, on the second floor right, where they put all the foreigners, presumably so that it made it easier to wire them up for sound. Charlie was also pleased to see the late night girls at the bottom of the stairs, right by the elevator, sitting in the chairs, smoking and opening and closing their legs slowly in case you didn't get the point. They looked sensational, and if he were truthful, he felt a little needy. But he had never paid for it, believing that with a degree of low cunning you could always get it somewhere else for free. So he waved a little wave and they waved back, thinking what kind of a jerk is this, and he went up to his room lonely, but no lonelier than you would be if you woke up a couple of hours later with twenty-two-year-old Sonia surveying you like a ruin while she cleaned her teeth with the tip of a purple fingernail.

First call, as always, was to Buddy.

'Etta told me to be expecting you,' Buddy said in his low, smoky voice. Charlie wasn't delighted to learn this but he let it pass.

They'd worked together for so long that Charlie had forgotten Buddy's last name. In his address book he was just Buddy, a veritable on–off switch – either 'There is problem' or 'There is no problem.' 'Problem', in Buddy's parlance, tended to mean that the course of action Charlie proposed might involve loss of life. 'No problem' meant that Buddy saw a way to lower the risk from lethal to manageable. This time, when he sat down under the blue awning of Moskva's outdoor café and studied the image Charlie handed him, giving special attention to the uniform, searching the epaulettes, looking for signs of a unit, he didn't say anything. This assignment seemed to go beyond the available categories of Problem, No Problem. Charlie was aware that his request – 'I want to find this guy' – didn't exactly add up. For one thing, where was Jacek? Why did he want to find someone if he didn't have a crew? If he was asking to locate some guy in a special unit uniform, heavy-set, with that particular mid-distance stare in his eyes, Buddy reasoned, it was going to be a war crime story. They'd done them before.

Charlie did not think it was advisable to let Buddy know where this was headed. He wasn't too sure himself. He had Jacek's parting words at the airport in his mind, and that gave a good general indication, but the operational details were still fuzzy. There was not what you would call a plan. Buddy, always discreet, looked at the red patches on Charlie's hands and did not ask questions. He could make the necessary deductions. Charlie had seen action down at the front and he'd seen something that left him strange and disconnected. It was also obvious that the picture Charlie gave him had been taken from output shot down there. So certain things added up and Buddy seemed to take the assignment for granted. This is what he always did. What Buddy ventured, after giving the matter some thought, was that he knew some guys. What kind of guys? Buddy shrugged and winced slightly. Guys.

So Charlie looked at the girls walking by the café and thought how glad he was to be back in Belgrade, while Buddy called his guys on his cellphone. Charlie didn't know the language, but he could tell that Buddy was getting somewhere.

Buddy was thin, withered even, and older than Charlie, with the air of a lapsed or defrocked professor. Once, years earlier, they had talked late into the night, and Charlie remembered that it was all Gadamer this and Marcuse that, and Buddy seemed to shed years and become the type of eager, hopeful Marxist who used to

93

meet foreigners in the '70s and talk about socialism with a human face. Now all that was gone and it had left nothing behind besides good diction and a choice use of language. Somewhere along the line, after the wreckage of an academic career, he had spent a few years in New York, in Brooklyn to be exact, but exile had not suited his nature. 'In shit is better', is all he would say about why he came home, although Charlie believed he had gone with every intention of staying and had been defeated by ordinary things, like living in a language that was not his own. And there had been some business with a Suzanna, if Charlie's memory served, who was much younger and got into Fordham Law School, so the story went, while Buddy languished at home in Brooklyn, listening to short wave radio. So Buddy came home, speaking perfect English, a little more mournful than before and a good deal older, just as his country took its suicidal plunge. 'Timing was perfect,' he said once. 'I leave and country is fine. I come home, and we are conducting experiment in mutually assured destruction.'

The one unreconciled resistance to English in Buddy's syntax was the dropping of definite articles. It was always 'problem', not 'the problem'. Otherwise his accent was New York perfect. Indeed it was a little too perfect. It didn't seem entirely trustworthy to be so fluent, to pass in and out of another language and leave so little trace of your own. He even asked Buddy about it once. 'Why is my English perfect?' Buddy pondered the question. 'Because English is primitive compared to our language.' Then he smiled and showed that amazing row of long, yellow teeth. Still, perfection raised suspicions in Charlie's mind. People who were perfect in English usually turned out to be spooks. But it would

94

be pretty imaginative recruiting if Buddy turned out to be one. As he watched Buddy with the cellphone cupped to his ear, nursing the cigarette that hung from his lower lip while his eyes scanned the crowds, Charlie thought he was wrong not to trust him. Or rather, he could trust Buddy as far as he could trust anyone. He felt dangerously detached, looking at the girls in jeans strolling by as if they were all on celluloid in some dull late night movie, rather than in the sizzling sulphur light of the street lamps. He didn't like this feeling of detachment, and he wanted it to stop, but like a state of advanced drunkenness, it wouldn't go away when you wanted it to.

Come to think of it, Buddy *was* OK. There had been that night on the highway in '92, during the Drina clearances in '92, when they were stopped by the Tigers at the checkpoint. They pulled everyone out of the Jeep and into this shit-smeared interrogation room in the station house nearby. They'd given Buddy the real treatment. 'It is normal,' Buddy said to Charlie under his breath when the drunk waved the gun about and said he would fucking kill everyone, fucking everyone. What Buddy meant by normal was that the swearing was a giveaway. Real shooters don't swear. This guy, sweating, eye-rolling drunk, wasn't dangerous, just unreliable, so Charlie kept thinking this is normal, and the drunk waved the gun about for the benefit of the boys lolling against the back wall of his office. Creeps like that always go for the local speaker, and they had gone for Buddy. This one had English. 'They fuck your mother? That's why you work for them?' 'They pay me,' Buddy said. 'What do they fucking pay you?' He gave him a number.

'What's your fucking name?'

Buddy gave him his name.

'So why this shit bag calls you Buddy?'

'It's my nickname.'

That's when he hit him. Jacek lunged, but the guys at the back had their hands on him and sat him back down hard.

'Don't get smart with me, shit bag.'

It took three hours for the asshole to sober up, three hours for the toxicity in the room to dissipate and for everyone to agree cheerlessly that it had been a misunderstanding. They got Buddy back into the Jeep, which had been stuck by the checkpoint, surrounded by Tigers wearing black garbage bags over their fatigues to keep off the rain. The Tigers raised the barrier and let them through and Buddy went silent as the smoking wood fire in the barrel by the checkpoint died away in their rear-view mirror. He stayed silent right through the next four checkpoints as they passed out of the active zone. He didn't even smoke a cigarette, though Charlie had offered him one. Yeah, Buddy was OK.

After talking with his guys, Buddy's plan was this: go south to this particular town on the municipal bus, spend time in a bar that Buddy knew and wait till some guys from the unit showed up to drink. Then get them to talk. Why this town? Well, mostly because the special units were stationed there and maybe some of them would talk. The reason they might talk was that the only known uprising of reservists had been there too. The boys came back from the zone, on leave, and went to the local press and said they wouldn't go back, they were sick of it. They even organised a demonstration in front of the party headquarters. So, Buddy reasoned, one of them might finger the guy Charlie wanted to talk to.

But the plan, such as it was, was risky. The organs

would pull you off a bus if they found you heading there. But then they could do the same here, if they found you talking to anyone in uniform. So Charlie would have to make himself inconspicuous and play Buddy's idiot brother or something and say nothing for a hundred and fifty miles of two-lane blacktop. But it could be done. It was good calling it a plan, though both of them knew it didn't deserve the name. They had to get an informant, they had to get lucky. It was obvious to them that they didn't know what they would do if they *did* get lucky. 'It is an improvisation,' said Buddy. Charlie peeled off a roll of dollars, Buddy palmed them, and they were in business again.

The good thing about him, Charlie realised after he'd got back to his room, was that Buddy never asked the motivation question. He did not say: Charlie, what is the story? What are you doing? This praiseworthy reticence was the result, Charlie judged, of all those years as a fixer for foreign outfits. They came in, they had stupid ideas for stories, usually stolen from a competitor, and Buddy never asked why. He had allowed luxuriant growth in the 'They don't pay me to think' side of his character. The result was mostly attractive: for example, he didn't chatter in the crew van, didn't volunteer dumb ideas and he didn't smoke all that much either, just slumped staring into the distance, occasionally telling a joke about a girl he knew in the town they were passing. The jokes had a certain charm in that Buddy enjoyed presenting himself as the hapless victim of one weasel-like blonde after another, although it was doubtful there was much truth to this persona. But there were sides of him that could be irritating. Once Charlie had come to town to track down a refugee story and they wasted a week discovering that the massacred refugee children, the innocents put to the sword, were all a mirage. Instead all they'd found was a drab motel on the outskirts of town, hung with laundry in the corridors, where the massacred children had turned up, safe and sound. It was funny, at least later on, how they had stormed through the motel, with Jacek irritably slashing the laundry lines aside, furious that the kids were actually there after all, grubby, tired, bedraggled and unharmed. The look in Buddy's eyes had said he had known it all along.

Charlie had worked with fixers in a lot of places, and none of them had this princely refusal to anticipate those disasters willed by his employers. It was scorn, not laziness, Charlie decided. Disasters willed by others, Buddy was prepared to fix. But if a team wanted to fuck it up, Buddy had concluded, it was not his job to stop them.

Charlie's working assumption was that this time – especially after six assignments or whatever it was together – Buddy would decide to warn him if he saw trouble coming. Though when he thought about it, he might know when trouble was coming faster than Buddy. He had not told him the whole story, and so there were bound to be some bad moments ahead, when Buddy discovered what he was in for, but on mature reflection, Charlie felt Buddy wouldn't back out. He couldn't say why exactly. It had something to do with the silence that had come over Buddy after the incident with the Tigers. Through the long miles of the night that followed, as they drew up to one checkpoint after another and Buddy sat staring straight ahead, you could feel his hatred for these people and what they had done to his country. Hatred like that was a lodestar. You could set your compass by it, or so Charlie supposed.

But, as he turned out the light in the Hotel Moskva, it did strike him that one of the commoner mistakes in life was to suppose that conviction was catching, to suppose that if you felt something with cold fury, Buddy – or anyone else – would feel it too.

Charlie rarely dreamed but he dreamed of Annie that night. He had wanted to call her from the hotel room, but he hadn't, and also couldn't now, he realised. He had been thinking of her as he drifted to sleep looking at the curtains eddying in the breeze as the city slowly settled and slept. When he saw her in the dream, it was so vivid that he wanted to call out to her. They were at the island, and she was getting into the small steel-frame outboard. She was maybe four and she had her life-jacket on, and she got into the boat carefully, the way he had taught her, first one hand then the other on the thwarts and no standing, just sliding down into the seat. She was wearing jeans and that red top and the toenails on her bare feet were painted light green. When she was seated, in the back, she was looking up at him and her hair was tied in two bunches. She said something to him, maybe calling him to get into the boat, but he couldn't make out what it was. But it was morning, and he knew they were driving over to the marina for bread and fresh coffee, and they had the whole day ahead of them. When he woke the curtains by the open window were still, and the city was momentarily silent and in darkness.

TEN

There was a war on, after all, and it wasn't smart to look like a foreign national on buses heading in the general direction of the front line. So he played Buddy's silent, possibly idiotic brother all that day, as the bus, one of those fume-spewing monsters, plied its way south, through one long village after another. There was a guy in the seat behind who had the look about him so they said nothing, not even when the bus stopped at a gas pump and everybody got off for a smoke and a leak. Even after the guy with the look stepped down at a town halfway, they didn't talk.

The windows were open, it was a bright spring day, and the curtains were flying around, and Charlie was thinking about municipal buses in Greece, half a life-time before. The Norwegian girl wore a straw hat, and he only knew her first name, and they travelled together for most of the day, conscious of the hot line of their bodies vibrating against each other. She would be fifty now, and he might not recognise her in the street. He wondered whether she remembered the old monk on the donkey they had seen at dusk riding through the lemon orchard. He wondered how she would remember the scene on the beach in the dark when they were naked and she had said he could, so quietly, just like that, that he didn't believe it at first. Then she added "But you have to come out before' because she didn't have any protection. So he did, and she had been a tight fit and it may have hurt her, though he didn't know and she hadn't said. She was a big-boned, wide-hipped girl with acrid white skin and freckles everywhere.

Afterwards they had gone to sleep in the upstairs room at the taverna on the beach. In the middle of the night, a drunk had burst through the door and fallen on his face on the bed across the room. They waited to see if he would move, and when he didn't, they decided to leave him where he was, breathing heavily, face down in his clothes. The next day when he woke up, his first words were in English: 'Who the fuck are you?' He turned out to be a cook from Macclesfield, the taverna owner's brother, home for a holiday. He wasn't altogether pleased that his brother had double-booked his room. His name was Spiro and he looked at the pretty blonde girl, holding the bedclothes up at her chin, as if Charlie was the luckiest man alive. Which at that moment, he was. The memory of it was so strong that Charlie began laughing, and the old lady with the kerchief in the next seat looked at him oddly, and so did the man with the busted blood vessels on his nose, who was reading the official newspaper. This was fine, of course, because Charlie was playing Buddy's idiot brother. And only idiots laugh for no good reason.

He was still in a good mood when the bus put them down at the depot in the southern town where Buddy said they were going to find the reservists. It was exactly what he had expected, though, as Charlie realised, few places surprised him any more. He had reached the age his father used to warn him about, when surprises just get fewer and fewer. It had the standard items for a town its size: old style imperial barracks, a baroque church that was shut, a yellow and white party headquarters looking out over a neglected, paper-strewn park with children's swings, a closed newspaper kiosk and the Hotel Sport's neon sign just coming on as the light drained away like dirty water in a tub. You couldn't imagine living in a town like this, but then that was your problem. The inhabitants probably thought there was no other life anywhere else, though there weren't many of them about to ask.

A dump, Buddy said as he surveyed the scene. On the other hand, it was the one place that had said no to the war. The reservists had formed up in this square, straight off the buses from the front, and they had smashed the doors of the party headquarters. This was to the credit of the town, Charlie thought, since it was the head-quarters of Second Army Group, and lived off the military, especially the bars where the soldiers drank off hours, like the one in the Hotel Sport, where they now proposed to spend – as Buddy gloomily put it – 'rest of our lives' till someone showed up. What they would do if no one did was not clear. They didn't have a Plan B. This had to be the bad guy's town, Buddy said, since the shoulder flashes on Charlie's still were from Second Army Group, Special Operations.

They drank a few beers and listened to the jukebox, though naturally there wasn't a country and western song on it to save Charlie's soul. So there was nothing to do but let the listlessness of the place seep into their bones. A few guys with short-cropped, Army-style hair came into the bar, eyed them suspiciously, drank up and left. 'This is terrific,' Buddy said, beneath his breath.

It was now moonless and dark outside. A silver Merc, one of those big heavy diesels, dusty from the road, wheeled into the square, and paused purring in front of the bar. The driver, whoever it was behind the tinted glass, had both of them in plain sight through the bar window. The machine stood there, and then slowly, wheeled off, rubber crackling over gravel. Buddy decided it was time to take a walk. The barman nodded. There was another place, he said, five minutes away. 'You should try there.' Buddy nodded. They hadn't asked.

The shutters were up on the long low rows of houses on both sides of the street, and thin oblongs of pale light from the televisions inside played through the shutters on to the sidewalk. It seemed that everyone in town was watching television and quite possibly watching the same thing. As they went past each house, Charlie could piece it together, glimpse by glimpse through the shutters. It was official television, lots of hearty accordion playing and big women in peasant clothing thumping around some studio. The people would have watched anything else had they been able to afford one of those foreign dishes. Whenever the editorial writers and other deep thinkers tried to portray the regime as serious Big Time Evil, Charlie always thought of the incorrigible mediocrity of its official television.

'Charlie, level with me,' Buddy said, head down, kicking the gravel as they walked.

Charlie said nothing. The reality was he didn't know what he wanted. Just find the bastard. But then?

'There could be problems.'

'Which it is your business to anticipate.'

'Your guy is Special Operations. Nobody is going to talk about Special Operations.'

'Since when did that ever stop you?'

This was how Charlie thought he would manage it, simply by provoking Buddy into remembering that miracles were his business.

'I know someone,' Buddy said, though why he hadn't said so earlier, Charlie didn't understand. Buddy knew someone in every one of these small towns. Someone had to mean a girl he had slept with once, or a man he done a favour for or had been in a car with on the road to the front, or had been shot up with somewhere. Their names and phone numbers were all in a scuffed cardboard-covered address book he kept in a vest pocket, 'next to my heart', as he put it. In this case, it was a local radio reporter, who lived behind the shutters of a small house, up one of the cobbled streets off the route the bus had taken into the town. Local radio was a good bet: during the reservists' demonstration, a reporter from the local station had gone down to the crowd in front of the party headquarters and had broadcast the whole thing – which was why anybody knew about it at all. The reporter was still in jail.

She opened the door and she didn't display any of the excitement that girls sometimes showed when Buddy turned up. She stood there, hand on the door, and smiled without surprise at Buddy and then gave Charlie a once-over, lingering on his eyes. There was noise from the radio and smoke rising from a cigarette in an ashtray, yellowed lighting from an overhead bulb and brown plush furniture, an unmade bed, a plastic screen behind which you could see a bathroom, and some of her underwear on a line over the sink. Anna or some such name. Charlie wasn't paying attention. She might have been twenty-five, and her colour wasn't all that good, pale like smoke. Why did they all look like this, these girls, with neglected black hair and that smoky complexion and look of resentment, as if you, a perfect stranger, were personally to blame for how their life had turned out?

She curled her bare feet beneath her on the sofa and studied the picture he gave her for a second, biting a fingernail. She looked at Charlie but he didn't see why he should give anything away. She didn't ask where it was taken or why Charlie was interested.

It was obvious she knew him. She said something to Buddy and then she looked at Charlie again and said 'the Colonel'. She nodded noncommittally and took a drag from her cigarette. So now they were looking for the Colonel.

She knew him, Charlie reasoned, because it was a small town, and a small unit, and at his level, he would be one of the kings.

Charlie couldn't figure out what else she might know and what she would be willing to say. There might even be something between her and the man himself. Or between her and Buddy. They were talking, not looking at him, and so anything might be happening. As she smoked and dropped the picture on the pile of newspapers in front of the sofa she might have been wondering what it would cost her to tell Charlie more. Such thoughts were passing through Charlie's mind, though he knew he couldn't really anticipate anything. Sustained attempts at anticipation turned out to be pointless or depressing or both.

He wondered how far she could be trusted. He couldn't make anything out from the way she moved the hair off her face and tucked it behind her left ear or from her thin smile as Buddy laid out his line of goods. In his business, Charlie was always trusting people. It was never exactly trust, of course, more a matter of playing the odds. She would be doing the same thing. If he was exposing her to danger so what? It wasn't his business to protect anyone. They were all adults here.

As the smoke thickened around the single light bulb above his head, and he watched Buddy talking to the girl on the sofa, Charlie had one of those moments of decompression when the point of it all – this journey, this story, whatever it was – seemed to be escaping him. What did these places mean to him now? These rooms with stained wallpaper, these local reporters and other people's wars. He was sick of it. He studied the poster of some long-haired singer in front of him and the Nike one on the other wall that said: Just do it. What he wanted to do was to go home. But there wasn't one to go to.

These senseless and abrupt drops in his internal barometric pressure came and went without warning and they made him feel that whatever he was doing was an entire waste of time. When they were happening, he felt that he had been emptied out by a life of following stories. He had done all this too many times, working a source in a dirty room in some place he didn't really care about. He felt all this but he also knew – this was the only benefit of getting older that he had ever noticed – that this moment would pass, and that he would recover momentum. Because momentum, after all, was all there was.

'What do you want him for?' the girl asked, in good English. She looked at him, evenly, drawing in the smoke, waiting to exhale.

Buddy shrugged, as if to say, I tried explaining, but no good.

'He killed a woman I knew. I want to talk to him about it.'

He hadn't meant to say it, or at least not yet. He had not said as much to Buddy. So it was Buddy's turn to look surprised.

The girl gave out a smoky laugh. 'Just like that?'

Charlie smiled back. 'Why not?'

Why fuck around with this? he thought. Why not just say it? It seemed to work.

She uncurled from the sofa, slid her feet into a pair of mules, grabbed a coat and the cellphone in front of her and said, 'Let's go. I show you. We find out where he is.'

The place they went to was the 'cultural centre' of the town, an old inn from the horse and cart days, with a stone courtyard and a dribbling fountain in the middle of it, trestle tables around about and a few blinking coloured lights around a small dance floor. It would have been fine, had there been any life in it. Apart from a couple of boys with close-shaven heads trying to make time with some girls in tight trousers and push-up bras, the place was empty.

'It's better in summer,' she said and threw herself down at a table by the fountain, beckoning to the waiter. He brought them some beer and Charlie wondered what they were doing there.

'He is sometimes here,' she said. 'It is his brother's place.'

So there was a brother. And if a brother, then there must be a blameless mother and a father and God knows who else, Charlie thought. These creeps had parents. He might even have a wife, and a daughter the same age as Annie, for Christ's sake. A real human being, in other words. But why should he care about that? It was all just sentimentality. What kind of life had you lived if you were surprised that killers led lives just like you and me?

What else was a man who set a woman alight supposed to be? He would be a human being like all the rest.

Charlie peeled the label off his beer and Buddy and the girl watched him.

'What kind of a story is this?' she asked.

'There might be no story at all,' Charlie replied with an even smile. 'I just want to talk to him.'

'And why would he want to talk to you?'

'Because if he doesn't, he'll go to The Hague.'

This thought had not actually entered Charlie's head until that moment. He had never taken The Hague seriously. But he was pleased to have improvised this threat and so he was smiling when she said, in a soft voice, 'He will kill you first.'

This also seemed to be Buddy's opinion since he nodded and gave Charlie one of those looks that said, 'Listen to her, even if you don't listen to me.'

'How do you know?'

She chose not to answer and simply gave him a challenging stare: a twenty-five-year-old woman confronting a man twice her age.

Charlie shook his head. 'He won't kill me. He doesn't want witnesses around.'

'What witnesses?'

Charlie pointed at the two of them. He smiled. They didn't.

'Shit,' Buddy said.

'You don't seem to realise . . .' she began.

'What don't I realise?'

'He did the ninety-two clearances down the Drina. The Omarska operations.'

'Nothing would surprise me,' Charlie said equably. They were in bluffing mode, and so he was bluffing. He'd had no idea, of course, that the Colonel had this kind of history, that he was a specialist, an old hand at the business. The Omarska operations had been really something: the dynamiting of the mosques, the mass eviction of the women and children, the men locked in that long cattle barn, the skeletal misery of those naked bodies, and the shaming fear in every man's eye. Charlie had been there. With Jacek and Buddy, in fact. They had won a prize for the footage, if his memory served.

'Leave him to The Hague,' Buddy whispered. 'Be stupid with your own life, Charlie. Not with mine. Not with hers.'

'Fine. Leave. You've done your job. Now go.'

But it was too late for that. She looked up and nodded at a man just coming through the door.

'The owner,' she said.

He strode over to their table, and she rose and let him kiss her once on each cheek. He was a big man, in starched white shirt and neatly cut slacks, maybe forty. He was handsome in a muscular kind of way, with pepper and salt wiry hair and the healthy colour of someone whose circulation is good, who sleeps well, who skis in the winter and plays volleyball on the beach in the summer. He was talking to the girl for a moment or two, and Charlie didn't know if it was business or something else, couldn't tell what kind of tab they were running with each other. Then she introduced them. Charlie could see that she was telling him that Charlie and Buddy were friends from the city and he could see that the owner didn't believe a word of it. But his hand was out. Charlie shook it and nodded. Buddy spoke for both of them. The big guy smiled, but kept his eyes on Charlie. Obviously, Buddy wasn't getting down to business, so after it went back and forth for a while, Charlie took advantage of a pause to say, very distinctly, in a way that formed a moment of silence around it, 'I'm looking for your brother.'

It struck Charlie that the big man didn't need a translation, but he waited for one anyway. Buddy obliged.

The big man surveyed Charlie, as if from a distance, and then he came quite close. He put his finger on a button of Charlie's shirt. He didn't pull it. He just rubbed the tip of his finger around it. Then he said something very softly. He stood back and smiled agreeably at the girl and Buddy and went back inside.

'I don't need a translation,' Charlie said, as they stood up to go.

'Yes, you do,' said Buddy.

They were under the street lamps outside the cultural centre. The music was floating through from the dance floor. The silver Merc they had seen before made another pass, slowing down as if the driver was taking a look, and then speeding away with a fluid change of gear. The girl looked at him and tossed her cigarette away.

'His brother will kill you, if you ever come back here again,' she said.

'Well now we know,' Charlie replied. It seemed clear to him that the girl was working for the Colonel or his brother and that Buddy had made a serious error of judgement. But who cared? They had got to the shooter first day, which wasn't bad, compared with other stake-outs he could remember. Now the question was: how long would it be before the Colonel made his next move?

'Nice talking to you, whatever your name was,' Charlie said to her in a hard voice. She gave him a long look and returned inside.

Buddy and Charlie walked back to the Hotel Sport, through the deserted streets. It had grown cold. The plane trees were bare, the branches black against the light of the street lamps.

'You don't know what you're doing, Charlie,' Buddy said in a tight voice.

'True enough,' Charlie said. 'I could say the same about you. At least we found the bastard. First time. I knew you could do it.'

'Fuck you,' Buddy said cheerlessly.

Charlie wasn't happy that his humour wasn't appreciated. In fact, he began to feel lonely as the silence between them persisted. It was then that he told Buddy the story, as they walked through the darkened town. There was nothing else to do, and Buddy was hurt and angry. Maybe frightened too, and Charlie, who wasn't frightened, didn't want him to be alone with his fear. He tried to take Buddy through the whole story. He tried to make the flick of the lighter as real as he could, the way the flames caught her clothes and how she began to run and the smell of her flesh and gasoline and weight of her body on his as they rolled on the ground. Charlie even showed Buddy the scar tissue on his palms, as if to prove that the event had really occurred. He wanted Buddy to understand what he barely understood himself, namely that she had impinged, penetrated, entered – perhaps the only one who ever had – the small space he kept between himself and the entire world.

He tried to tell Buddy of the ridiculous hope they had entertained, Jacek and him, of saving her, of doing something right for a change, and how the crushing of that hope had set Charlie on this course. Though this wasn't the only reason. The reason lay deeper, in how he had witnessed so much in a life of reporting and had done so little, how he had never saved anyone, and needed to now. But saving wasn't the right word.

'So guilt maybe?' Buddy cut in bitterly.

Charlie shook his head. He didn't feel especially guilty. The deepest feeling escaped words, and he fell silent, just walked beside Buddy. What he could not say was that his life had never been redeemed by a single thing, though where this yearning for redemption came from, he could not understand. Since when did life required to be redeemed? he might have asked at any other time, but not now. He wanted to convince someone, anyone, of the necessity of what he was doing.

But Buddy was not convinced.

'Do you suppose that this is only bad guy in my country? Or in world? Do you think that fixing him fixes everything? How stupid can you possibly be?'

'I want to fix one thing.'

'And what's that supposed to mean?'

'I don't know.'

'You don't *know*! Jesus Christ, Charlie.' Buddy was disgusted and walked ahead on his own.

Charlie usually knew what to say to anyone's disgust, but this time he couldn't find the words. So he kept quiet the rest of the way back to the hotel. All he could think about as he walked along was a film he had seen once, not a very good one, about this Greek guy whose father had been tortured and murdered when the military was in power. The son returns from exile twenty years later and he sets off to find his father's murderer, on some picture-postcard Greek island. He has this idea that he is going to kill him, and he brings a gun along. All that Charlie could remember about the picture was a long scene, where the son climbs a blistering white road upwards to a house at the top of a village where the murderer had gone into pensioned retirement. He turned out to be an old man sprinkling goat manure from a red plastic bucket on some tomato plants in front of the house. It was the guy all right – his name was on the mailbox, plain as day. The son watched the old man watering his plants, watched him wipe his runny nose, and then he kept walking to the top of some cliff and threw the gun into the sea. The ending seemed fine at the time, but it wasn't how Charlie felt about things now. He didn't care about revenge. It wasn't revenge he wanted. What he cared about was the burning woman and, for her sake and for his, going through to the very end, wherever it was, no matter what.

And what did that mean, exactly? Where would it all lead? Charlie didn't have a clue. Just a feeling that closed in upon a scene in which he and the Colonel were on opposite sides of a table, and the Colonel had to give an account of himself. A reckoning. That was what he wanted. Not vengeance, just a reckoning. So that the Colonel would understand what it really means to snuff someone out. So that Charlie would understand. So that the distinctions, the clarity, that life requires would be restored. Something like that. And maybe more. He wanted the man to feel fear, wanted him to know what being burned would feel like. That was it. A laying on of hands. The flame of recognition and shame would jump the gap between one soul and another. Something like that. One way or the other, a kind of religious occasion, a righteous moment.

He caught up with Buddy and tried to put his arm around him, but Buddy pulled away.

'You are a danger to yourself,' Buddy was saying. 'And you are a danger to me.'

'I don't want to be a danger to you, Buddy,' Charlie said.

'I don't need your good intentions,' Buddy replied, flicking a butt into the arc of the street light by the entrance to the Hotel Sport. 'I just want to get out of here.' But it was too late to get out of there, at least that night. The next bus wasn't until 7.30 the next morning. The bartender doubled as the night porter, and he handed them two keys.

The rooms upstairs at the Sport were eloquent witnesses to the sexual life of a garrison town: from the stains on the orange carpet, to the hair oil on the headboards, the declivities in the mattress, and the holes in the curtain, half-hanging from its hooks, as if someone on her way down to the floor, in some biting and scratching mouth to mouth with a soldier, had grabbed at it to hold on, caught it and dragged it with her to their coupling on the floor. There was a rancid smell to everything, mouldy decay, deep in the fabric, sunk into the stained tiles in the bathroom. Buddy was at the end of the hall, and Charlie heard him visit the toilet on the landing, and then turn the key in his lock. Charlie opened the windows and kept his clothes on. He didn't want his skin on these sheets.

There was no phone in the room, so there was no one to talk to, and it wasn't that late, so there was nothing to do but lie and watch the light of an occasional headlight playing on the torn, lopsided curtain. For the first time in weeks, it struck Charlie that he had been in the grip – like the guy in the bad Greek film – of an old myth. Telling the story to Buddy had broken the spell. He realised that he had been stupid to fall for it. All the redemption there could be was in a story, but it had to be a good one, a new one, and the one he had fallen for was old and tired. Who believed in vengeance any more? Or reckonings, for that matter? Plenty of people did it, of course. Vengeance went on every day. But who actually believed in it? Who believed you could make the world right? To believe in an eye for an eye, a tooth for a tooth, you'd have to believe that there was an order out there, which it was your business to restore.

Get serious, Charlie thought. Vengeance was just a dignified name for a crime and a reckoning was just a piece of righteous foolishness. The world was wrong and it was not your business to fix it. Knock it on the head, Charlie, he said to himself. Knock it on the head. Go home. See your daughter. Move out on your wife, if you have to, make a change or two. Keep on going. Find Etta. Tell her you are sorry. Tell her you were an idiot, out of your mind, loco. Bare your soul, or whatever can be found of it before it is too late. The woman on fire was dead. She had been remembered, which set her apart from all the other corpses Charlie had seen in his life. He would not forget her. He had honoured her in his way. He had tried. Jacek had tried. It was enough. Enough.

He said the word aloud into the darkened room. 'Enough.'

He heard the door open, a subtle sound, the catch caressed back, by a fingernail smooth against steel. Charlie was reaching for the light but he didn't get there in time, for the figures – there were two of them – had crossed to the bed, and lifted him, by throat and belt-buckle, to an upright position against the wall in one single, breath-sucking move. He couldn't see their faces, and they might have been hooded, because in the split second that it took, their faces gave off no light or reflection. They held him off the ground, thumb in Adam's apple, against the wall and then one of them struck him a single blow right in the centre of the stomach. The thumb against his Adam's apple let go and he felt himself fall, the door slam shut, and a pain exploded from the centre of his guts in the interminable moment that it took for him to pull breath back into his tortured chest.

Next morning, when Buddy couldn't get an answer he put his shoulder against the door and it flew open and there was Charlie propped up against the wall, a spewed trail of vomit on his clothes. Charlie's head was nodding against his chest and when Buddy knelt and took his face in his hands, Charlie opened his eyes but he couldn't talk. Buddy cleaned him up, and pulled away Charlie's hands, held claw-like against his guts, moved back his shirt and inspected the spreading blood bruise on Charlie's upper stomach just below the diaphragm. Charlie looked up at him and tried to speak. Buddy said, 'Charlie, shut up.'

Buddy heard the bus roll into the hotel courtyard, and he reached down and tried to get Charlie to stand, but his legs were rubbery and he just sat down on the side of the bed. So Buddy put Charlie's arm on his shoulder and his hand around Charlie's waist and pretty well carried him down the stairs to the front lobby. The guy behind the desk – the same one who would have let the goons in – rose and gave Charlie a quick look that expressed more satisfaction than was wise. He was also foolish enough to say that there was a night's bill to pay. At this, Buddy reached inside his jacket and pulled out a pistol. The guy behind the desk rather comically raised his hands as if the gun required them both to pretend that they were in a cop movie. Buddy, with Charlie under his arm, slipped the pistol back into his inside jacket pocket and they made their way out of the hotel to the bus. Buddie lowered him gently into a window seat, while the baffled passengers looked on. He paid the driver and then sat down, and as a final flourish, gave a little wave to the guy at the hotel who was standing on the steps.

The bus was rolling, and it didn't make any sense to keep pretending to be Buddy's idiot brother, so Charlie just whispered, 'A gun?' Buddy nodded and said, as if he never went anywhere without one, 'A 45-calibre Glock.' He kept looking out the window. Of all Buddy's miracles, this was the greatest. Charlie, in a delirium of pain and relief felt like kissing him. A gun. And more than a gun, what the gun meant. Buddy had known all along what they were getting in to, and while the gun hadn't exactly been of much use, it had saved them from at least one hotel bill, and most of all, it proved that Buddy was in for the long haul.

That wasn't the only surprise. Buddy waited until the sight of one man lifting another into his seat had worn off on the rest of the bus and everybody went back to looking out the window or listening to the radio, and then he said, very quietly, 'He is in Belgrade. She phoned. I can't figure out why.'

But Charlie knew. She had done it for the same reason as Buddy. So that the woman on fire would get respect. So that one guy, just once, would understand what it means to treat someone like garbage. She had known this. She had seen it in Charlie's eyes. Charlie could see her now – she had finally come into focus – with her bare feet, nails painted purple, the smoky complexion, and that clear questioning look as she let the photograph drop on to the table between them. Why had he ever thought she would do anything different? People were amazing. It was a sign, definitely a sign, though Charlie realised, as the pain in his chest took over, that he was not really in his right mind. He closed his eyes. Buddy sat looking out at the dark and newly turned furrows in the fields.

ELEVEN

When he got off the bus, Charlie was pleased to discover that he could walk. In fact, he and Buddy walked the whole way up the hill to the Moskva. It was a bright and cold afternoon and Charlie liked the smell of coal and cigarettes in the air, liked how a woman ahead of him was moving inside a long black leather coat, and the way her calf muscles contracted and tightened as she ascended the street. He still hurt, but the pain was in retreat, pulling back from the whole of his body to the fist-shaped bruise below his diaphragm. Buddy was smoking, and he pulled the smoke into his lungs as they climbed the steep street. There was something remote and calm and clear about him. Because of the Glock, because of everything, Charlie thought that Buddy was the greatest guy in the world.

Buddy did not share Charlie's euphoria. He took the blow to Charlie's middle for what it was: a final warning. He also took it as a sign that he would have to think for the two of them, since Charlie didn't seem to understand the kind of danger he had put them in. What was it about Charlie? It would be pleasant to suppose that he was simply fearless, but this was not the case. He had seen Charlie afraid. The new fact was his appalling lack of interest in self-preservation. Some of the cunning and, watchfulness essential to survival had gone missing and, as a result, Charlie was a danger to himself and to anyone else in his vicinity.

Buddy didn't say any of this, but Charlie sensed what he was thinking from the bruised sort of silence he maintained the whole way up the street. When they reached the hotel, they repaired to the bar at the back and the flame-haired barmaid of a certain age who'd been there since Charlie started coming to the Moskva brought them an espresso each and a glass of plum brandy. It was just the thing for his stomach, fire that went all the way down and burned away the big knot inside. He had another.

'So now we go for him,' Charlie said.

Buddy downed his brandy with a shake of his head.

'I am going to put you on a plane,' Buddy said emphatically. 'It is not possible to have you running around this town. You are just crazy.'

'I won't go,' Charlie said, smiling.

'I will have you sedated. I know guys. You will be carried on to plane, and you will return to wife and child and all will be well.'

'I won't go,' Charlie repeated, with his most engaging smile.

Charlie could tell that Buddy was going through the motions, doing due diligence in case anyone blamed him afterwards. Charlie was not fooled. After the gun Charlie knew it was a sure thing. Buddy was his. Buddy even smiled to acknowledge honourable defeat.

'You are going to your room and you are sleeping,' Buddy said. 'All day.'

'You're giving the orders?'

Buddy nodded.

'And you?'

'I make phone calls.'

Charlie didn't believe he would sleep, but in fact he fell asleep in his clothes, out cold on his back. He woke, sore and dry-mouthed and lonely. His watch said 10.45 p.m. He'd been asleep about five hours. Somebody was knocking on his door.

They had a passkey: two men were in the room before he got down the stairs from the loggia. A third stood waiting in the hall. The one who did the talking had thin blond hair, a slight trim body inside a suit and a face that was impossible to remember except for watery grey eyes. Charlie didn't like standing there in his socks, with his hair mussed up on the back of his head.

'You will come with us,' Watery Eyes said in English.

'What's your problem?' Charlie had been in these situations before. It always paid to spin things out, even when it was obvious that he didn't have any room to manoeuvre.

'Visa problem.'

'What about my visa?'

'You are journalist, but you enter as tourist.'

'For this you wake me up at night?'

'Shoes, please.'

'Who are you?'

'You know very well.'

'You might be anybody.' Which was true in this town. Federal. Secret. Militia. Private. Who knew? Charlie studied his possibilities. Flight was not one of them. Resistance wasn't either. Yet he knew that they didn't want him struggling in the corridors. There were a few other guests, after all. So they wanted it done quietly.

Watery Eyes kept his hands in his pockets.

'Shoes,' he repeated. 'Pack everything.'

'Why?'

'You are leaving.'

Charlie pointed up to the loggia where the bed was. 'Shoes,' Charlie said. One of the men followed him, and the other one waited downstairs.

So he had hit pay dirt, Charlie thought to himself. The Colonel had the connections to get Watery Eyes into his room, just five hours off the bus. Not bad, when he thought about it. Charlie even felt a faint stirring of journalistic pride. He had got close enough for the whole system to stir into life, for it to close around him like some ocean-floor bivalve closing around its prey.

Charlie packed his bag and sat on the side of the bed and took his time lacing up his shoes, while a man stood over him to make sure he didn't have anything interesting in mind. Charlie had nothing interesting in mind. He felt dead tired and overwhelmed with the pointlessness of his situation. They would have his passport, and they had him. It was over. He knew who did it and it didn't make any difference. It was over. Charlie wasn't the kind to take satisfaction in having tried. In his business, you either had the story or you didn't. You either aired it, or you didn't. E for effort wasn't worth a thing. Getting kicked out of the country wasn't even a good career move. For he had been fired. Or suspended. Or whatever.

And there was the woman on fire, dead and unre-deemed, killed not just by the Colonel himself but by everything you could see in Watery Eyes's expression, the same sort of predatory indifference. It occurred to Charlie, as he contemplated journey's end, that she was the one person he really cared about. As he tied the last shoelace and stood up, while the hood picked up the bag and gestured for him to go down the stairs, he wondered whether he might still have a card left to play.

The possibilities were to get out into the hall and start yelling in the hope that some foreign passport would hear, or that Buddy – if he happened to be there – might do something. But if you started yelling, they might just hit you and carry you down the back stairs. And Buddy might not hear. Then again, Charlie thought, rapidly revising his earlier idea, Buddy might have had a hand in this. The thought was depressing, but Charlie wasn't so sentimental as to be taken by surprise. People thought he was one of life's hopeful fools, and he had gone a long way exploiting this misperception. But Charlie could easily envisage how Buddy would rationalise a deal with Watery Eyes. Buddy would think it was in Charlie's best interests to be bundled on to the plane or the bus with a mug on either side to keep him from moving and then be dumped on the border. Buddy had to live with these people. Charlie didn't, so what Buddy did to keep alive here wasn't his business. Still, the idea that Buddy might have set him up made Charlie sick.

As they marched him along the corridor towards the fountain that disconsolately pissed away, all night and day, by the second floor elevator, Charlie noticed that the usual working girls had been cleared off the chairs where they lounged by the elevator door. So the corridor was empty. But he drew comfort from one thought. By coming quietly, he had lulled them into making a mistake. Instead of taking him down some freight elevator at the back, they were taking him right down the main steps to the lobby.

This was how, when Charlie reached the lobby and crossed it and was walking, framed by mugs on each side, and Watery Eyes following behind, holding the bag, he managed to trip on the second of the grey marble steps leading up to the street-level entrance, where their car was waiting. It was an innocent-looking mistake, and he didn't make a production of it. He only went down on one knee, but it caused them to make a second mistake, which was to lift him up by the arms so that anybody could see he was being bundled out of the hotel by force. Charlie didn't know whether anybody had caught his signal, but as it happened he had created just enough disturbance at the door for three people sitting at the rear bar drinking at a table with a view of the lobby to see what happened. One of them was Buddy, and the other two were Etta and Jacek.

They were smart enough to remain motionless, though it was hard, especially for Etta, to sit perfectly still, after the glass entrance door swung closed behind Charlie and they heard car doors clunk shut and the black BMW drive off. They finished the brandies, took an elaborate amount of time paying, so that the flame-haired waitress wouldn't feel inclined to report on their interest in the recent departure from the hotel.

'I'll get the embassy,' Etta said when they were outside.

'I'll go to the headquarters,' Jacek said, knowing where it was, since he had been questioned there once himself. 'You stay out of sight,' he said to Buddy, who nodded and disappeared.

Etta found a urine-soaked phone box and managed to push enough change into it to make it work. The night guard at the embassy answered on the fifteenth ring. She talked him past the procedures in his binder, the ones that ought to have had him hanging up. It was her job getting people to do more than they were authorised to do. When the third secretary, dragged from sleep, came on the line, there was a lot of 'Can it wait till tomorrow?' but Etta said it couldn't. She knew how to lean gently but unrelentingly on officials, until they could begin to see the cost of hanging up and doing nothing. The cost, Etta implied, was being fired.

She walked the steep hill down to the headquarters, past the Defence Ministry, past the sentries, feeling the police cars slowing down to observe her. She had a map in her pocket, so she knew where she was going, and she put her faith in her basic meticulousness, which included having studied the streets of a city she had never been to, on the flight from London, so that she could find Charlie if she had to. Of course she was frightened. Why not? she said to herself. What else should she be? That was how she dealt with fear. It was a matter of saying, 'Why be surprised? Why not admit it fully?' Then you wouldn't think it was weak or ignoble. You would just think, this is how it is.

The right thing to do here, she reasoned, was to make a lot of noise, make it costly to deport a foreign journalist. The more noise, the better. Like the Plaza de Mayo women banging their trash can lids with spoons in front of the President's palace in Buenos Aires. She'd seen them on TV and she'd always admired those women, who campaigned to find out where their sons and daughters, husbands and lovers had been taken, how they had made noise, day and night for years, enough to reach through prison walls, enough to make the world notice. She wanted to believe in the power of noise and she began humming to herself, 'A People United Will Never Be Defeated', something she chanted in a demonstration once, until it seemed ridiculous and died in her throat. As she came to that cheerless granite pile squatting on the height looking down on the highway to the airport, she told herself that she and Jacek were not playthings here. They had options, cards, chances. She told herself that it was a third-rate dictatorship, brutal but not classy, and that she didn't need to be afraid of these guards in the sentry boxes. But she was also a child of socialism – a Young Pioneer herself – and she had memories of the times when these places had real menace. She couldn't quite overcome those feelings that came from a Communist childhood of being intimidated into silence by the brutality of buildings like this one.

They weren't going to let her in and the stiff in the guard-post was pretending he didn't even see her media pass till Jacek, who had got through, came down the steps. They made a fuss, they held her back, but Jacek just took charge, and there was something implacable about him that made the guard think it would be easier to let them deal with this lunatic inside.

Inside the state security office Etta and Jacek sat together, side by side, on a bench against a wall, beneath a fly-spotted bulb, and looked at the dreary paraphernalia: posters with official regulations, tacked to the wall opposite, the corners torn and curling; the dirty linoleum floor; a series of unmarked doors, and a high counter behind which sat a sergeant in uniform who surveyed them without interest. It was cold and she shivered and pulled her coat around her.

Jacek went up to the counter and tried it a number of ways. Etta could see that he had been trying for some time. His language was passable and so he said 'Are you deaf?' then 'Are you stupid?' 'We know he's here, so let us see him', all of which were met with the same reply.

The sergeant was neither deaf nor stupid, but intelligent enough to see that a game was being played and that he had a part too – which was to insist that a journalist, named Charles Johnson, from London was not in their custody.

Etta watched Jacek with fearful admiration, wishing that she could be left to persuade the sergeant in a softer, yet more effective way. But she deferred to Jacek's scornful fearlessness, and the way in which he managed to turn something risky into a game, which allowed both the sergeant and him to keep it all from getting out of hand.

Eventually, Jacek came back and sat down beside her and they waited.

'We wait,' Jacek said to the sergeant.

'So I see,' the sergeant replied and went back to his paperwork, with a small smile.

Stand-off. If they stayed there, it might be difficult for them to move Charlie. If they stayed there, the embassy might show up.

They didn't speak, and they didn't have to, even though today was the first time that Etta had ever seen Jacek face to face. It had always been on the phone before – the booking, contracts, equipment rental, flights – and occasionally Jacek would pass her on to Magda, because Jacek could be vague on details and Magda never was.

He looked older than his years, and the lines on his face and the tiredness that came over him in repose tightened her heart, because it made her think of Charlie too, how they were old men, getting older, in a young man's game, and how they knew this but kept trying to exploit the diminishing advantages of experience, knowing all the while that those were diminishing, and that one day, they would be old and sidelined, full of experience that no one would want.

She could see what Charlie liked about Jacek: no wasted words, no unnecessary forms of politeness, self-containment and quiet when at rest, fierce economical action when in motion, and all the while this wolf-like gaze, taking in the seedy desolation of the room as if he was framing it up in his viewfinder.

He might be thinking: What exactly is she doing here? but she didn't care, or didn't care to explain. What she was to Charlie was her business alone, and she was part of the story now.

The embassy showed up about forty-five minutes later in the form of a small, dishevelled woman in her early thirties with round glasses, who came in with a file under her arm, and one card outstretched for the sergeant and another one for the two of them. It said that she was a third secretary, political. Etta was glad about that. Political had more muscle than consular.

It was rather impressive, Etta thought, how this small woman managed to embody a government and to initiate a formal demand for access to a detainee, according to such-and-such a convention guaranteeing consular access to all detainees in a signatory's power. She cracked the words out in the sergeant's language, but with an official cadence that, even if it was the mumbo-jumbo of sovereignty, carried a certain authority. They could make out that she was telling the sergeant the government was unhappy, the ambassador was unhappy, the country would be unhappy, the whole world would soon be unhappy. It was a good show, all round, especially coming from a tired, anxious woman impersonating the authority of Charlie's home and native land. Even Jacek seemed to enjoy the way this flow of words caused the sergeant to rise from his seat and disappear through a door into a back office, carrying the third secretary's card.

'That was good,' Jacek ventured.

She did not reply, just sat down beside them and they waited in silence. Her distaste for journalists, for the mess they got into, the mess they left behind, the mess she had to clean up, was so palpable that neither Etta nor Jacek bothered to say another word. Etta listened to the sounds of the building, the surge and rattle of the water in the pipes, the clank of doors somewhere, a garbled voice behind a door, then long silence when she could only hear the blood in her ears. He would be down below them, and she tried to imagine the cell, but only the usual images came to mind, a spy hole, whitewashed walls, a single chair, all under fierce light, and none of it, she knew, *his* cell, the particular place they were keeping him.

It was a lesson she had learned somewhere in her life, to fight free of any images she had of a thing – in this case a jail cell – because it would make it impossible for her to know the thing itself. She wanted to listen to the way Charlie would tell it – and he would tell it, she fiercely believed, he would tell it, and she didn't want anything to get in the way of his telling, and her listening.

When she looked up, a compact athletic man in a suit was standing in the far doorway behind the counter, looking at her with watery grey eyes. He had been there for some time. Etta felt herself being inspected and she did her best, with the return of her gaze, to deny him any satisfaction. His gaze moved from her to Jacek and then to the woman from the embassy.

'In here, please,' he said, gesturing to the third secretary.

When the door opened again, forty minutes later, she was in the lead, with Charlie just behind her, carrying his bag. When he saw Etta rising from her seat, pulling her coat around her, with her mouth opening into a smile, and Jacek breaking into a grin beside her, he shook his head in disbelief.

'I'm getting too lucky,' Charlie said, and he meant it, as he kissed Etta and smelt the fragrance of her skin and hugged Jacek. He was too lucky. It couldn't go on like this. He ought to be in the cells or on the plane out of here, and he wasn't, because they were there, because they had raised the alarm. It just couldn't go on like this. And Watery Eyes had made another mistake, which was releasing him at all.

When the third secretary had them out in the street, she said, curtly, 'See you at the airport tomorrow morning. Nine o'clock.' And she took his passport out of the file. 'I will hold on to this until then, if you don't mind.' Charlie nodded and with that she got into the embassy car and drove off.

'We've got plenty of time,' Charlie said.

Etta said, 'It's over, Charlie. You must be on the flight.'

'Sure,' Charlie said. 'I need a drink.'

They were back at the Moskva just in time, for the first chair was going up on the tables, but Jacek managed to persuade the flame-haired waitress that they wouldn't be long, only one drink. Charlie didn't want to talk about what had happened, not there, and all he said was that they hadn't laid a finger on him. But it wasn't strictly true, Etta could see. Something had happened down there. You could feel it in the way Charlie drank and the way he looked at her, with a kind of empty desperation and even shame, and then looked away. He said that Watery Eyes kept asking him what he was doing down south and Charlie had said that since they knew what he was doing it didn't make any sense to keep asking him.

When he said this, he smiled, but when Jacek asked him what he wanted to do now, Charlie said, looking at Etta, softly with the sound dropping down to nothing, 'Kill that son of a bitch.' As he said this, he had the look of a man who first wanted to take her upstairs.

Etta saw that he was slipping away into that hard, exalted place where he did harm to himself. She could see it in his eyes, in his brittle amiability and his reluctance to keep still. She could see it in his longing for her too, since it was wild and had more to do with fury than with desire.

Charlie was just enjoying the last burn of the alcohol down his throat when Buddy walked in. Charlie assessed him, the short beard with the strands of grey, the old leather bomber jacket, the cigarette in the corner of his mouth, the neat flannel trousers which didn't go with anything, and he thought it wasn't possible, no it wasn't possible that Buddy would be working for Watery Eyes. In fact, he concluded that Buddy hated Watery Eyes just about as much, if not more, than he did and that Buddy was looking for the same shot as him.

He got up and took Buddy outside. 'I've got six hours.'

'It is enough. Address is not far,' Buddy said and pointed to a small black car parked across the street. Charlie had just got in, when Etta ran out after him. She had thought Buddy would stop this, and for some reason Buddy wasn't stopping anything.

'Charlie, for Christ's sake.' She reached through the

window and grabbed his hand. Jacek was behind her and Charlie knew he thought the same thing as Etta.

'I just want to talk to him,' Charlie said and he covered Etta's hand with his own.

'Charlie, don't be ridiculous. There will be police there.'

'We'll find a way.'

'It is not good to be arguing like this,' Buddy said evenly from the driver's seat, looking about to see who might be watching them.

Charlie looked at Etta, at her face in the car window frame, and he said, 'Etta, I'm tired of being fucked around. Do you understand?'

He could tell she did understand. He could also tell that it didn't change her mind. He pulled his hand free, and the car drove off.

TWELVE

The address that Buddy had was on the other side of the river in one of those apartment towers built when there was a country and it had a future. Buddy was driving towards it with intensity, both hands on the wheel, the smoke from his cigarette blowing into his face. Charlie sat hunched up in the front seat and took the cigarette out of Buddy's mouth, ashed it in the butt-filled tray and then stuck it back between his lips. The car was Buddy's mobile office, as he called it, with back issues of some review he had edited in the old days when there was a culture and he was an intellectual and everyone was young and had books all over their back seats. The car was a pretty good image of where they stood with the competition. Watery Eyes had his BMW, and all they bloody had was a Lada, short one windshield wiper.

Watery Eyes would do his job, Charlie was sure. So the Colonel would be waiting for them. Fuck it, Charlie thought. After those hours in the basement interrogation room, he was glad to be in the car, in the dark, with Buddy at his side. There hadn't been any rough stuff, just the same old questions, for which they already had answers, and the unspoken inference that in this fluorescent basement, with a water bucket, a tap, a drain in the centre of the floor and two figures in the background whose faces never came into the light, anything could happen.

Except that it hadn't. Watery Eyes hadn't reckoned on Jacek, on Etta, on Buddy and on the third secretary from the embassy. Thanks to them, Charlie had a few hours of grace. What he understood about grace was that you never deserved it. It wasn't a reward for his lunatic obstinacy. It came upon you unbidden, like the light of the moon. So here he was on a clear, still night in a sleeping city, having been mysteriously granted enough grace to reach the end of the road. For that was what it would be. The hunger would be sated and he would never pursue anything again with the same all-sacrificing intensity. For the first time in his life, Charlie found himself reconciled to the future and to the path his life had taken. He sat hunched up in Buddy's Lada, feeling something between elation and contentment. He had gone the limit. '*Que sera sera,*' he said. In his mind's eye, he could even see Doris Day herself, in the grainy black and white television of his childhood, singing the song with her witless and touching good cheer. It was laughable, and Charlie did actually laugh, softly to himself, a low chuckle that made Buddy look over at him and shake his head in disbelief.

Buddy's mood was different. It registered in the way he gripped the wheel, the way he smoked. He seemed furious that he was locked into Charlie's fate and that Charlie didn't seem to care one way or the other.

'I am doing this, Charlie, so that you will never say I was coward.'

He said this with such uncharacteristic solemnity that

Charlie smiled. Cowardice had never figured in Charlie's view of Buddy. He felt a surge of tenderness for his ruined face, and the moustache yellowed with tobacco, and he wanted to tell him that he trusted him and knew him to be courageous. But he didn't say it, because he wasn't sure that it was all true. What *was* true was that Buddy had the Glock in his leather jacket pocket, and, like the true professional he was, the butt handle was sticking out for all to see. Charlie reached over and pushed it down out of plain sight. Did Buddy actually know how to use it? It didn't matter. It could make a noise. It could scare somebody. That would be enough. The gun was in the category either of a comfort or an embarrassment, but either way, it was coming along.

'You're OK, Buddy,' Charlie said.

Over the bridge, down the ramp, off to the right, Buddy drove down into a parking lot at the foot of the block where the Colonel lived. 'A lot of officers live here,' Buddy said, surveying the building. So it was a real hive of wasps, Charlie thought, and if their wasp needed help, the others would come swarming. Finely splintered auto glass crunched underfoot, and black audio tape, torn out of somebody's car deck, drifted across in the breeze, picking up a sliver of light from the moon. Some lights of the ten-storey tower were still on, while from others lower down, the blue flicker of televisions glowed. It was cool, and Charlie's hands felt cold. He put them into his pocket and he gripped his tape recorder.

They weren't exactly sneaking up on him so there was no point, in Buddy's words, playing *Jemsbond*. The Colonel's name was on the board by the doorbell and so they rang it. Buddy went to the intercom and said his name, but whoever was on the other end did not answer. Instead, the electric lock on the glass door clicked open.

It had been too easy, and both Buddy and Charlie found this unnerving. On previous assignments, they had staked out guys for days and had never managed the slightest breach in the wall. There would be dogs, or cops, or disinformation and all trails would go cold. All the way through this one, there had been a strange lack of resistance. True, he had been knocked around and arrested, but he and Buddy had kept on coming, and now the Colonel was apparently letting them come the final distance. He had been released, Charlie believed, on the Colonel's order. So he was walking into some kind of a trap, but he reasoned it couldn't be much of a trap if he knew that it was. Anyway, if it was, there was nothing he could do about it now. He couldn't turn around, walk to the Lada, shrug and say, Buddy take me back to the Moskva, take me back for one more night with Etta, take me back to my life. That was the sort of sensible behaviour Charlie knew he would regret for the rest of his life. He knew exactly why. They had made a mistake. They had fucked with him. They had misunderstood who he was. Now they had to find out who they were dealing with.

Buddy and Charlie both reached for the elevator bell at the same time and thought how stupid they must look. They listened to the machine's sepulchral rattle as it descended from the upper floors, and then felt it settle with a crunch, and open, waiting to take them upwards.

They ascended in silence, not wanting to look at each other, knowing it wasn't even worth planning what to do. They simply had no idea. 'You cover the door', 'I'll do the talking', anything they would have said would have come from some cop movie, and was too stupid to quell the fear that had taken hold of both of them.

When the elevator juddered to a stop on the tenth floor, and they stepped out, light was coming from a door ajar at the end of the corridor. They went towards it, single file, and Buddy crossed the threshold first. Charlie, still in the hallway, heard a voice stop Buddy in his tracks.

'The gun,' the voice said. 'Empty the chamber and put the gun on the floor.' Buddy did as he was told, letting the bullets drop on to the polished wood, and then dropping down himself and giving the gun a little push so that it spun away. The voice said something else and Buddy repeated over his shoulder, 'He wants to *see* you.'

As Charlie came around the door-frame, he heard the man say, 'Empty your pockets,' and when Charlie stepped into view, he could see that he was armed, framed against the picture window which glowed from the lights of the city. His face was backlit and in shadow, but it was the man all right, legs apart, gun pointed, taking the measure of Charlie. So Charlie said – because he knew the safest way was to avoid any unannounced gestures – 'I am going to reach in my pocket, and I am getting my tape recorder. I have no weapon. OK?'

'OK. Then sit down.'

'Where?'

Charlie said it as challengingly as he could, because an instinct told him to push back a little, see whether there was any give, any room to manoeuvre. There didn't seem to be any.

'On the floor, there, where you are standing.' The English was good, and it made Charlie rush to fill in the blanks – an embassy posting, a spy job in London or

Washington – but the blanks stayed blank and Charlie knew he was in a room with a man he knew next to nothing about, except for that gesture with a lighter, that casual flick of the wrist, the backward glance, the walking away, the unreachable, unteachable disregard.

Charlie considered turning the tape recorder on before he slid it across, but he discarded the idea. It had a tell-tale red light and made a sound, and this guy wasn't exactly stupid. So Charlie pulled it out and as he went down on his knees he shoved it across the floor.

'On your face,' the man said, getting up from the chair.

'Why?' asked Buddy.

'Why not? What choice do you have, gentlemen?'

This was true enough. They lay face down on the floor. He approached, tapped the hall door shut and stood over them. Then he patted them down. Charlie felt thick fingers running across his body, snaking along the rim of his ears, spreading out through his hair, down between his legs, calves, ankles; even his shoes were given a feel. From where he lay, Charlie caught his first real sight of the man: forty-five to fifty, big, muscular, a plain white T-shirt, running trousers, bare feet, salt and pepper hair, like his brother, trim gut, and a service revolver trained at Charlie's head while the free hand patted him down. Their eyes met: and whatever Charlie had expected – fear or anger or even triumph – was not there. The eyes that took him in, face down on the floor, were neutral, professional and entirely unafraid.

He was doing it right, Charlie could see, confident enough in his ability to take on two strangers at night. Even with a warning, even with preparation, he was doing well. But there was a puzzle here, Charlie realised. He could have left everything in the hands of Watery Eyes. Most of them did. You never got close to war criminals. They let the police handle the foreigners, and contract killers handle the domestics, like Buddy. So Charlie was uncertain about his luck, but it did occur to him that the Colonel had planned this all along.

The Colonel stood back and said in a calm and uninflected voice, with a tinge of irony, 'So you are a journalist. Interview me.'

Charlie and Buddy turned and sat up. He was motioning with the gun towards a sofa behind them.

He was smiling.

Which was a mistake since the smile was too perfect: too intelligent to be a smirk, but too pleased with itself to be anything other than a display of infinite self-regard. It was a mistake because it restored Charlie's self-possession, enabled him to think again, to feel what it was that had brought him here.

'Could we get some light in here?' Charlie said, as he sat down on the leather sofa.

'No,' said the Colonel, taking his seat, revolver on his right knee, legs apart, body straight, looking at them.

Behind him to the right were bookshelves and there was a hard line of light underneath a door leading to another room, a military shield or unit emblem, perhaps, hanging on the other wall. The apartment seemed spacious and spartan and there didn't seem to be any female touches about. But you couldn't be sure of anything. There could be someone else in the other room behind the door. Charlie couldn't tell. The only light came from the moonlit sky, still hours from dawn, and from the glow of the city across the river. Just behind the Colonel, there was a glass door, left ajar on to a balcony, and cold air from the outdoors streamed around their ankles. The Colonel was a few feet away. You could hear him breathing.

'Are you the Colonel of Second Army Corps, Special Operations?' Charlie began.

'You know this already,' he said.

'Were you in the Drenica valley a month ago?'

'You know this too.'

'Prijedor? The Drina valley back in '92? I am told you were there too.'

'Why not?'

'Yes or no.'

'We are not in The Hague here. All this "yes or no" is for prosecutors, and you, Mr Johnson, are not a prosecutor.'

Again, that smile, a glimpse of white incisors in the gloom.

'What kind of a story are you writing, Mr Johnson?'

'Yours.'

'There is no story,' he said.

'Forget stories,' Charlie said. He didn't want to play around any longer.

'So what are we doing here? And you, Mr Savic, what are you doing with this man?' the Colonel said.

'He is my friend,' Buddy replied.

'And why the revolver?'

'Because I wanted to kill you,' Buddy said.

The Colonel laughed softly. 'Belgrade intellectuals,' he said. 'For possession of this weapon, you will do three years.'

'You will arrange this personally?' Buddy said.

The man nodded and shrugged, as if to say: 'Yes, if it gave me pleasure. If I wanted to.'

Buddy, on the sofa beside him, felt Charlie's body

stiffen and lean forward. He was as tightly wound as a hunter with his prey in plain sight, just there, through a clearing, waiting for a clear shot.

'Listen to me,' Charlie said. 'There was a woman. In the Drenica. A month ago. I was there with a crew. We have tape.'

'Yes, Mr Johnson, I saw your report.' And the Colonel gestured into the gloom as if to say that he had sat there one evening in this very room, watching the nightly atrocity footage, lifted off the international network feeds, only in this case it had happened to be his unit and his atrocity, him in body armour and holding a cigarette lighter in his hand.

It had been one of Charlie's hopes that he would surprise the man. But there were no surprises after all. The Colonel knew everything. It didn't seem to matter that it had all been seen, that his secret was known and that Jacek's images had captured it all. There was something in the face in front of him that told Charlie the Colonel was even glad to have his very own home movie.

Charlie had been wrong about everything. He had thought the Colonel would have forgotten the woman, among all the others who must have passed through his hands or the hands of his unit in the years of war. Charlie had come to make him remember, and he remembered everything. You could see it in the face in the darkness. So now he had to feel it. He had both to remember and, for once in his life, to feel it.

Charlie's voice did not rise, it fell to a whisper. Every word came out with a pause between. 'You. Set. Her. On. Fire.'

The face across the darkness was without expression. The gun on his knee did not move.

'So what I want to know is why. I'm not a prosecutor. I don't give a fuck about justice. You'll never go to The Hague. But me, I just want to know. Why.'

Again, the man in the darkness did not move or speak. A silence ensued. There was the murmur of traffic noise from the open door of the balcony.

Charlie could wait. In the instant he had said the word *why*, he had felt everything come clear, the whole insane exercise making sense. Why. He wanted to know why her life turned out not to matter at all.

'You think she was garbage?'

The Colonel said nothing. Instead he reached down to the floor, all the while covering them with the gun, and picked up the tape recorder. With his free hand he pressed Record, and placed it on the floor between the two of them. Now there was a tiny red operating light and a new sound in the darkness: the slithering of audio tape through its silver gate.

'Why?' he replied. 'You ask why?' He smiled again. 'Because she was sheltering you.'

She *had* given them shelter. Except that she wasn't offered a choice. They had burst through the door and into the rootcellar, before she even opened her mouth. They had never exchanged so much as a word. But that wouldn't matter. She had not betrayed them, and for that she had paid.

'You torch her for this?' Charlie was leaning forward.

'So the others learn from her example, Mr Johnson.' He said it quietly, as one professional to another.

Charlie said nothing. Her example. The others. The way he said it stopped all thought.

'The unit you were with sent a signal. We picked it up. You made an obvious mistake, Mr Johnson.'

Buddy couldn't understand the look on Charlie's face, its utter blankness. It seemed to Buddy that Charlie had not anticipated this questioning and that now he was staring down into an abyss.

'And what were you doing there, anyway? When I saw your report on the television, I laughed. You proved that the terrorists had a base four kilometres inside our area of operations. You risk your life for this? You risk *her* life for this?'

You risk her life for this. It is not what you intend. But it is what results. No one ever intends the consequences, especially when the intentions are good.

The Colonel said one more thing, quietly, as if stating a mere matter of fact, as if it were the most obvious thing in the world, a statement that could not admit of contradiction.

'Collateral damage. She was what you Americans call collateral damage.'

Charlie saw her face, her eyes, her mouth opening and closing, opening and closing, soundless: save me. He felt her breath on his face, her hands gripping his shoulders, the palms and fingers of his hand fused into her burning flesh.

'You talk about her like this?' Charlie whispered. He was so close now that Buddy could see the two men were within touching distance. He thought they might be there for a long time just breathing, and so what happened next was the last thing he ever expected. Charlie rose with a roar in his throat and lunged across the dark space, catching the Colonel's neck with the force of both hands. The two bodies crashed backwards against the glass door, on to the balcony. The glass shattered as it swung back and Charlie fell on top of him with his hands around the Colonel's neck, roaring between his teeth, making the sound of an enraged and tortured animal.

Buddy was on his knees, looking for the revolver, when he saw the Colonel bring his knee up, lifting Charlie's body into the air, while his hands chopped Charlie's grip off his neck. Buddy's hands found the gun just as the Colonel pushed upwards with his legs and vaulted Charlie's body up on to the waist-high railing of the balcony. Buddy was raising the gun when he saw Charlie, on his back, his head tipped backwards into space, his legs and trunk balanced on the railing, his hands struggling to right himself, like a bug on his back. He was gasping for air, looking up and Buddy was shouting but it was too late. The Colonel gave one last kick and without a sound, Charlie pitched wide-eyed into the void.

The Colonel stood up on the balcony, his white T-shirt spotted with blood, but the smile on his face was telling Buddy that really he shouldn't pull the trigger. Watery Eyes had entered the room and had his gun at Buddy's back. Then everything slowed down, in the long viscous time of afterwards. Buddy could hear the city sighing in the distance and at his feet the tape still slithering through the gate. The red light glowed. The Colonel bent down and turned it off. Watery Eyes reached out to take it, but the Colonel handed it to Buddy. 'Take it. It's your interview.'

THIRTEEN

One minute Etta was in the car park wrapping her hands around her elbows to keep warm, while Jacek was loping towards the building, the next she was running in the direction of the sound and the stillness that followed it. Afterwards it seemed a mercy to her that he had fallen feet first so that his head had been spared, as he lay there broken like a doll, eyes shut, unscarred and dead. She was kneeling beside him and her finger was still on the place at the base of his neck where she had felt for a pulse when Watery Eyes and his men came up and Jacek lifted her to her feet and took her away.

She did her job, as she always did, clearing the body from the morgue, working with the embassy to get the paperwork done for the flight back to England. She was the one who, with the help of the third secretary, did the deal with the authorities. Buddy would be released and allowed to return to the United States, it being understood that he would not discuss the case. Otherwise, of course, his ex-wife and his ailing mother, both obliged to remain, would face consequences too obvious to discuss. Buddy did not object and neither did

Jacek, and so Etta was the one who let the ground swallow up Charlie's quest. She conspired in the embassy's official story that there had been a tragic accident, and it did not surprise her that the local journalists did not dig further.

She accompanied the body home on the plane, watching how the plain box was loaded, and then unloaded at the other end. At the airport, she delivered it into the hands of Shandler and the others from the office who came out to take over. Elizabeth was there, composed but red-eyed, and in an airport lounge Etta gave her an account of what had happened and handed her Charlie's bag, the one he had left behind in the Moskva.

She did not attend Charlie's funeral because she had no standing there. It was a family affair. She did not want to see Charlie's daughter, and she did not want to see Elizabeth again. She did not want to listen to what others would say from the pulpit about him, neither their tenderness nor their valedictory lies. Jacek said he would go for the two of them. This, she said, was fine with her.

After the ceremony – a south London cremation – which she spent in her apartment, seated at the kitchen table, staring out through the blinds into the grey blankness of the London sky, Jacek rang. He said he did not want to intrude, but he was at the airport, and the flight to Warsaw was not full, and if she wanted to come, Magda and he would like her company.

She was there within an hour and sat silently beside him throughout the flight then drove with him through the dark Polish countryside, until the lights from the car picked out Magda in the drive of their farmhouse. Etta got out and allowed herself to be embraced by a woman she had never met. They stood in the darkness and thanks to the warmth in Magda's body, Etta managed to strangle the cry in her throat.

They put her in the same room that Charlie had used and she went to sleep looking up at the night through the skylight. She stayed for three days, quiet, replying when spoken to, obviously wanting to be there, but not wanting to speak, and since they didn't want to speak either, their silence was companionable and unquestioned.

Magda worked at her translations at the table with the view of the garden, and Etta sometimes sat nearby, reading and then putting her book down and staring through the window. It was May, and there was green grass and the beginning of leaves. The air was moist, cool and smelt of tilled fields. Their pigs were birthing.

She went out into Jacek's workshop and sat on a stool and watched him clean his cameras with the air hose and the fine brushes. It wasn't clear whether he was just going through the motions, or preparing for another assignment. But Etta didn't ask him, because Jacek might not have been able to tell her if she had. Jacek said Charlie had done the same, sat and watched him work by the hour when he stayed with them, and Etta received this news without expression. They did not have to say that he was still there, a liminal presence like the echo that remains when a gun has been fired.

He had chosen his redemption, and there was nothing to regret about that, she thought, except that it was also an act of desertion. One night, she stood alone in the bedroom, in her dressing gown, and she reached down and undid the belt, as she had once done, to fold him in, and then since the room was empty, as all rooms now were, she felt the full weight of her desolation.

She was leaving the next day, going back to work, she said. Dinner was over and they were all seated around the table in front of the fire when she said finally – without any preliminary – that she thought Charlie had been an innocent. Magda asked her what she meant, and Etta paused and looked at her wine glass, and pushed a strand of her blonde hair off her face and said that when she was eighteen, in her country, she had been raped. A family friend, she said, with no particular emphasis or irony, correcting herself, not a friend, a member of the family. Her mother's younger brother, Uncle Janos. Out of the blue, as they say in English. He still lived in the town where she grew up, and her parents never knew, and life went on as if nothing had happened. But that was why, she added, she left home, and why she had begun again. Magda reached out her hand but Etta gently shook her head as if to say that she wasn't looking for consolation. She looked at Magda calmly and said in that thoughtful and slightly accented voice, 'I do not want you to misunderstand. It was an experience that taught me that we live in a world where there are people who do this. Whether they understand what they do or not does not matter. Why they do it is not an interesting question. What matters is that they do it.'

Charlie, she said, was an innocent because he never lost his surprise at this fact about the world. He should not have been surprised. It was a mistake, she said, looking out of the window at the reflections of their faces and the black night behind.

Neither Magda nor Jacek said anything, though Magda put her hand on top of Jacek's as if to shield him from what was being said, as if she feared that Jacek might be a prisoner of such innocence himself. Whatever he thought, Jacek let her hand rest there, his eyes staring at the littered table.

'It was a mistake,' Etta repeated, 'to be so hopeful and therefore so angry when it happened.'

'What happened was wrong,' Jacek said.

'Of course,' Etta replied, looking at him with tenderness. 'Of course. But that is not the point.'

'Why did Charlie believe he could get an explanation? Why did he feel the world, this' – and her hands moved and made shadows through the light of the lamp on the table – 'should owe us any explanation at all?'

Jacek said that it was not the world that owed us an explanation, but men. One man in particular.

And here Etta rose from her seat and went to her room, returning with something in her hand. It was Charlie's tape recorder – just as Buddy had given it to her – and when she clicked Play, a red dot of illumination came between them on the table.

Of course she had saved it. What else could she have done? Return this monstrosity to a grieving and uncomprehending widow, these sounds of her husband's final seconds alive? Or jettison it, throw it into a bin at the Moskva, so that nobody would ever have to hear what she heard the night she played it alone? No, she could not do that either, for it would have betrayed Charlie, who, whatever else was wrong about him, had died for a certain truth.

So she had to play it, and she could only play it for Magda and Jacek because they were the only ones who would understand why listening was a necessary office of friendship and an act of witness to the love they had all felt for the man whose face, voice, touch of hands, smell of skin, was fading inexorably from their memories.

What they heard was this: the scrape of Charlie's

shoes as he shifted position, the sound of the Colonel's bare feet, Buddy, Charlie, and the Colonel breathing, city noise in the distance through that door opening out on to the balcony and human voices muffled, off-mike and distant as if under water. They had expected, Etta especially, that the tape would be a confession. They had not realised it only contained an accusation, the claim that Charlie had brought the whole calamity, the whole catastrophe of the woman's death upon himself. They heard the voice of the man who had escaped all judgement and they heard the calm certainty with which he pronounced his own self-exculpation, his ingenious escape from the trap of guilt and the accusations of memory. What they heard was an infamy and since infamy is mysterious, they listened in the rapt silence reserved for the greatest of mysteries. None of them believed the accusation, and none of them ever would, but the truth in it still carried, as the Colonel himself must have hoped, all its capacity to wound.

Jacek rose from his seat, shut the tape off violently at the point where the speaking stopped, and went out into the night air to be alone. This left two women, one who had loved Charlie, and the other who had tended his wounds, to switch on and hear for a last time, before Etta reached over and threw it into the fire, the final seconds of the tape, the avenging roar from the depths of his being, that was Charlie Johnson's last word.